Sol y Sombra

Steve Brown

First Published 2009 – Limited First Edition.

ISBN: 978-99932-0-688-0

Book design & Layout by Scott Dear

Published by Tiny Island with the assistance of BDL Publications Malta.

Printed by Gutenberg Press, Tarxien, Malta.

Contents

For Alice

GUN SHOP

Tacho and I first met one day in June, in the gun shop across the street from the Frontier Hotel. I was three weeks out of Cornell and had just purchased the ranch from my father. I was the boss now and I was cocky.

I had $410 cash in my hip pocket. I had won big at the Friday poker game in the room back of the bar in the hotel basement. I was on my way to buy my pistol.

The street was very hot, with no evidence of rainy season as yet. Waves of heat streamed up to the tin sky from the dusty cement sidewalk and black asphalt street. The crosswalk lines at the corner shimmered like a pair of dancing snakes.

I jaywalked straight across the street and stepped inside the gun shop door.

The long narrow shop was a downtown fixture. In the 1950's it sported a heavy glass door with the words "Quality Firearms" stenciled in gold script beside a long plate glass window.

Now the window was bricked-up behind rusty iron bars. A three-ring pawn sign hung over a cheap steel door with the single word "GUNS" crudely lettered above a faded red plastic "Come In We're Open" sign behind a tiny bulletproof window.

I remember visiting the gun shop as a boy with my father. Then, I stared up at the mounted deer, elk and antelope heads that lined the walls, and saw my reflection in heavy oak cases that gleamed with guns. Over the years, the shop's interior grew shabby. Posters replaced the taxidermy and the oak was gone; cheap fiberboard cases lined the walls and formed the counters. A stained runner covered the old tile floor.

A battered air conditioner rattled above the door and spat stale air on my neck as I entered. I stood in the doorway for a moment. Fluorescent light cold and blue as a gun barrel streamed up from display cases and down from the ceiling.

I was surprised to find another customer in the store, as downtown had seemed deserted in the mid-afternoon heat. I hid my frustration at having to wait. I stepped out of the air conditioner blast and pretended to study the rifles on the wall, but out of the corner of my eye I concentrated on this customer. I noticed a clerk slouching back of the pistol case halfway down the narrow storefront.

I had some to learn about pistols and my first impression of this customer was that he knew what he was looking for.

The clerk I ignored, but his customer piqued my interest.

He stood straight and he appeared strong. His hair was jet black and close-cropped; a clean straw hat rested on the counter near his elbow.

He was dressed like most men in this part of town on a summer day, white long-sleeved Western shirt with three pearl snaps at the wrist and one on the forearm; clean Levi's over good black cowboy boots. The boots were not new but were well-made and polished, the sort of boots you put on to go to town. Except for his skin color and his particularly erect posture, he could have been me. My age.

"Probably military," I thought to myself. What I could see of his deeply-tanned hands suggested a working man. "Not likely an officer," my mental checklist continued. "Mexican? Indian?" I hadn't been listening to the conversation so I hadn't caught an accent yet. I shifted slightly, still studying the rifles on the wall but putting my head in a better position to listen.

The first voice was the clerk's and it was not pleasant. "No way, José. You're not walking out of here with no pistol, not on my watch."

This further piqued my interest. I was after a pistol, but I had no idea what sort of documentation was required. My father had given me my guns in the predictable sequence, starting with my .410 shotgun on my tenth birthday and progressing through my .22, my 20 gauge and then my deer rifle in two-year intervals. These all hung on the gun rack in my bedroom, but my father would not allow a pistol in the ranch house.

Now that his office was mine, I intended to have a pistol like his, nestled in its holster on the shelf over my desk, the ammo in a locked drawer. I would load and carry it on the range as need be. I had the pistol I wanted in mind and I now had the cash in my pocket, won fair and square.

I quietly edged a little down the counter, fiddling with a magazine in case they looked up from their business, my ears peeled.

I heard the customer speak. He definitely had an accent but it was hard to place. He spoke softly but I have very good hearing.

His diction was clear, "As I see it, sir, you do not have that choice. Here is my driver's license and my birth certificate, and this," he slid a paper across the counter to the clerk, "is my honorable discharge."

The customer tapped lightly on glass. "The tag on that revolver says $389.99 and these are four one hundred dollar bills. In this town they don't get any greener."

"You see the firearm stamp on my discharge?" he queried the clerk. "You're familiar with this stamp?"

"That stamp don't mean shit to me, cowboy," the other man muttered, concerned that I was eavesdropping. I picked up the magazine and stepped back toward the doorway, turning my back on the pair. I positioned myself to hear the echo of their conversation off the back wall. I watched them in the cracked mirror at the end of the shop.

I knew the revolver with that price tag. A long barrel .32, it had a diamond-scored walnut grip and a straight-forward action with a small hammer that would not catch mesquite twigs when I rode through brush. The gun itself appeared rugged as sage; black brushed steel, it was a revolver you could drop in a water tank and then fish out, clean and oil and shoot straight as a die. The front sight was the size of my pinky. The perfect gun for a horseman.

"Damn!" I thought to myself. "The clerk's giving this guy a run around, and he has all his stuff in order. Maybe he'll get that pistol, maybe not." I considered my options,

"What do I want to see happen here?" I said to myself. I decided to take some ownership in this conversation.

I put the magazine down and sauntered over to the pair. "Is there a problem here?" I inquired.

"If there is it ain't yours, sonny," the clerk glared at me across the counter, his eyes expressionless as bubbles in a stagnant pool. "Speedy Gonzales here is the one with the problem."

The customer looked at me too. "Actually, Lopez is the name." He smiled and extended his hand, which I instinctively met and shook. My initial impression of his strength was confirmed. His skin was rough but soft and supple as soaped leather. "Tacho Lopez."

I nodded as he continued, "That's with a C-H." He raised one eyebrow a fraction. "Do I know you?"

"I don't think so," I replied. I introduced myself. I liked this man instantly. We both turned back to the gun dealer.

"Lookit, sonny," the dealer addressed me, "In case you didn't notice, your new pal ain't quite the same as us." He lowered his voice as if we were buddies in a barroom and Tacho was invisible. "Mexicans in this town need pistols like hookers need crabs. He ain't gonna buy no pistol in here. Especially on a Friday."

I almost reached across the counter to shake some sense into this little odious man. I caught myself in time and instead poked Tacho's Army document on the counter with my left forefinger.

"You idiot," I snapped at the clerk. "This guy carried a gun in the service so people like you could have stores like this. If he hadn't beat me to that pistol you'd of sold it to me, but you're out of luck, pal, 'cause I'm outta here.

I was set to stalk out of the store, but the clerk's disdainful look egged me on, "And one last thing, I'm not your sonny—my father hawks and spits better than you're made of. Ranchers like us have put money into this hole for forty years, but you're toast now."

My blood boiled and my hands shook.

To my great surprise Tacho burst out laughing. *"Caballero!"* he exclaimed. His dark skin crinkled and his black eyes sparkled as he regarded me fuming by his side. "It's just a pistol!" he stage whispered to me. "You take it!"

I shook my head, my heart still pounding behind my eyes. The store seemed way too bright. I stayed rooted to the floor.

Seconds passed. Tacho's laughter faded. His smile disappeared as he turned his attention back to the squirrel-faced clerk. "Okay, *bueno*," he said. "I think I understand you. Now you listen to me!"

Quick as a cat Tacho straightened up from the counter. He stood a good two inches taller than me. He folded his big hands and pressed his forefingers together and pointed at the man across the counter, who recoiled as if he had been struck, although Tacho had moved back smoothly as he straightened to deliberately keep his hands on his side of the counter.

His voice dropped a note and the expression on his face turned smooth and hard as a saddle.

"We Mexicans have this little saying, 'what goes around comes around.' The world turns and your number comes up snake eyes. Next time around, *babosa*, maybe you come back as a top quality cow horse, the kind my friend here would ride."

"One day you, this fine horse, you're way out on the range, eight hours from home, doing your job. But this day you have very bad luck. You step in a gopher hole and you break your ankle. You know you're dead, and the man on your back knows you're dead, too; and he knows the only right thing is to shoot you and end your pain. With dignity."

"This man, he cares for his horse. He's crying but he knows what he has to do."

Tacho unfolded his hands and touched his hip, mimicking reaching for a pistol. I stood transfixed. The gun shop clerk paled even further as he suddenly realized what Tacho was saying. The store seemed to grow ten degrees colder.

Tacho's voice dropped even further. His words crackled and the clerk heard them clearly, "But this man who you've carried, who you trust, he remembers he doesn't have his pistol to put you out of your pain. His pistol got stolen by some bunkhouse cowboy. Maybe pawned. Payday came. But, still no pistol after payday because of a little *cabrón* who wouldn't sell a pistol to a Mexican."

"So you, this quality horse, you lie there in your own shit for eight hours while this man walks out to the road. You lie there and gasp while your lungs fill with your blood."

"You watch a redtail hawk come and pluck out your top eye while the red ants crawl in your other eye, the one against the dirt 'cause you can't raise your proud head any more. The *javelina* tear your *cojones* off and when night comes you hear the bobcat slink 'round you and hiss."

Tacho hissed in such a good imitation of a bobcat that I felt the hairs on the back of my neck stand up. The clerk cowered.

Tacho didn't miss a beat, "This Mexican man who loves you—this man whose family bred horses on this range before that *cabrón's* crawled out of some swamp—he walks out to the road and hitches a ride to the Mission to borrow a pistol from his priest. They drive back. They walk out in the moonlight and the snakes let them pass. They end your pain."

"That horse's pain is *para tí, vaquero*. God has reserved those eight special hours just for you."

Tacho's face softened again and he winked at the clerk, who stood rooted to the floor. The air conditioner clattered. The door buzzed as another customer stepped in.

Tacho smiled his gentle smile and he touched my shoulder lightly. "Buy you a Coke, *hombre*? It's a hot one! Let's get out of this ice box!" He gathered his papers smoothly in his left hand, his hat in his right, and nodded to the new customer, a scrawny cowboy who came right up to the counter and greeted us all with a touch to his hat brim.

It was time to leave. I grabbed my hat and followed Tacho out to the sidewalk. He was laughing softly to himself and shaking his head. I followed him down the sidewalk to the shade of the Walgreen's awning. We sat down on canvas chairs at a faded tin table, and a pretty waitress brought us Cokes.

I felt a confusing range of emotions. My anger was still there, with some shame and confusion. But most of all I was curious. What had just happened? What came next?

Tacho had a faraway look in his eyes. We sat with our backs to Walgreen's, deep in the shade, the bright street quiet except for an occasional car or pickup stopping at the light and then moving on.

A mother with a couple of kids and an elderly woman, maybe their grandmother, sat around another table a few yards from us, sipping Cokes and laying out some cloth they had purchased, fingering the material and chatting quietly.

This time I didn't eavesdrop. I had enough to deal with right here.

I chose my words carefully, "What he did, that's illegal, right? They can't discriminate against you if you've got your papers, and no record?"

Tacho nodded. "Tell me about this ranch of yours," he replied, delicately changing the subject.

I was always ready to talk about the ranch. "It's the MW ranch, about 70 miles southeast, down in the Canciones. My grandfather built it up right after the turn of the century. He was in the first war and my dad was in World War II but other than that they worked the ranch their whole lives."

"I just bought my dad out with what money my grandfather left me, mine if I made it through college and wanted to stay in the business. My old man says he's going to work for me, but we'll see how that goes."

"I know your place some," Tacho replied. "My father's a part-time blacksmith and I think we've been out there. Off highway 88, about five miles past Cierrito Corners, back in the foothills, what, maybe 10 or 15 miles?"

"Yeah, that's us." I felt flattered. Maybe Tacho and I had met, as children watching our fathers on a Saturday. I remembered pumping the big portable bellows blacksmiths brought to our barnyard, feeding gnarled oak to their fires before the advent of butane.

Tacho continued. "I heard you bought the old McAdams place on the backside of the Canciones, too." He raised one eyebrow and gave me the look of appraisal I'd first seen in the store. "You're going to need a couple of hands if you're going to build that place back. Last time I was past there the adobe house was half gone and the fences were on their sides."

Now it was my turn to laugh. "Small town!" I replied. "News travels fast!"

"You know it. I spent the last four years in Germany and Viet Nam and I've got a lot of catching up to do too." Tacho's keen eyes slid across my college ring on the Coke glass and up my arm to meet mine.

"Look," he continued. "You took my back in there even though it was not your fight. That was good. Thank you. More than what some folks in your position would've done."

"But don't waste any anger on that fella. My grandmother, this little bitty old lady even the priest is scared of, she taught me how to deal with guys like him. You think he will sleep sound tonight?"

"Ha!" Tacho snorted.

"You go back in and buy that gun if you want it. It's a nice pistol and if you don't buy it some sorry *vaquero* will, and that, my friend," the big man paused for effect, "would be the real crime."

He finished his Coke and leaned forward on the table. His serious side surfaced again, "My friend, rainy season will be here next week. I'm looking for work and maybe what I have to offer is what you need up in those mountains." He gestured slightly with his chin toward the distant Canciones, rising blue as saint's robes through the heat shimmering off the sidewalk.

"What you got for horses?" he queried me.

I thought for a moment. I too had been away four years, a fact Tacho had picked up. I wasn't quite sure. I knew my favorite horses, but the rest, the ones the cowboys rode, were a blur.

I wasn't about to admit this, though. "We've got about twenty, mostly geldings, a half dozen mares. A couple of registered quarter horses but mostly just good cow horses. My sister has a mustang she got up in Nevada but no one else rides him; she's only home a couple of months in the summer."

Tacho rolled his eyes. "Women and horses," he snorted. "My sister's the same way. 'Don't you touch him,'" he mimicked his sister's voice. Except for the accent it could have been my sister. We both laughed.

I was definitely interested in his offer. "What you got?" I asked.

"OK, *bueno*," he replied. "I grew up on the Sunset Sahuaro Ranch out west of town. My old man's the wrangler there, and he blacksmiths some, as I said."

"I finished high school and enlisted in the Army. Cavalry. I wanted to be around horses. Horses are what I do;

it's been in my family's blood for four hundred years. Father Kino, you know the story."

I nodded. Everyone who went to school in the Southwest knew Father Kino, from their first-grade coloring books through their high school civics and history classes.

He continued, "Well, they sent me to Germany and for the first two years I was in horse heaven. I was blacksmith to the General and I lived with the horses, made sure they were pretty and agile on Sundays when the Corps rode them in parades with their swords, and all those big blond women waved." He took a deep breath and gazed off at the mountains in the distance. "*Ay caramba,*" he sighed.

I wondered if he was remembering the horses or the women. I decided not to ask.

"So then, the Army in their brilliance decided if I could fix a horse, I could fix a truck. They sent me to the jungle for two years. I was safe enough, *gracias a Diós*; never got out of this goddamn big garage. I learned how to strip down and rebuild jeeps and trucks and tanks, but horses? I didn't lay my hand on a horse for two years."

"My chance came and I was on that DC-8 before the ink dried. I've been back in town two weeks and I'm ready to work."

"I'm not going back to the chewy cholla; my father's job could be mine, but I can't deal with those dudes, not after what I've seen in 'Nam." He paused and smiled.

"Two more things."

"Oh, no," I thought to myself, "What's coming now?" I did not want this conversation to turn. I gave him my full attention.

"I will never ride in another helicopter. And, I will not eat a goat unless you cook it well done. Anything else, I'm your man." He raised that eyebrow again and his dark face crinkled as he smiled across the table.

I laughed as much with relief as at Tacho's familiar reference to Sunset Sahuaro Ranch. It was a famous dude ranch, known for attracting wealthy easterners who spent the winter there, bouncing on trail rides and swimming in the heated pool. Real ranchers called the spread "chewy cholla" because of the jars of bland cactus fruit preserves the dude ranch brought to the County Fairs and sold through their catalog. Our wives and mothers put up preserves, too, and they all laughed with each other while chewy chollas' jelly jars gathered dust on the shelves and theirs brought home ribbons.

I felt like a weight had suddenly been lifted off my shoulders. I knew our ranch; and after my four years at Cornell, I thought I knew everything I needed to know about cattle, but horses and vehicles had always been someone else's business: whose, I wasn't quite sure. I just knew my Jeep had gas in it and my horses were ready when I wanted them, the privilege of the owner's son.

But now I was the owner.

It suddenly occurred to me that I could hire Tacho. I had that power.

I had never hired anyone. However, I had taken Business Administration classes as part of my degree in Animal Husbandry, so I knew all about applications, interview techniques, strategies for grilling references and negotiating salaries.

"You're hired." I said. "When can you start?"

That was more than thirty years ago. Tacho and I are still working out the details.

WINDMILL TOWER

"Today when I woke up it felt like home," Sara stood on tiptoe on the narrow stool and shouted into the ancient phone. She grimaced and tipped the receiver away from her ear so I, too, could listen to the response.

Her mother's voice crackled all the way from New York. "Well it's not your home! Your home is here with us! I don't know what possessed you to follow that cowboy; he's probably tall and handsome and plays "Home on the Range" on his harmonica or accordion or some other God-forsaken instrument and you think it's romantic!"

"Have your fling if you must but don't be fooled. Your Aunt Gwendolyn got involved with a cowboy once and look how she turned out!"

I cupped my hands over my mouth and pinched my nose to stifle my laughter. Sara rolled her eyes and tipped the receiver back against her ear. I squeezed around her in the tiny pantry and hummed "Home on the Range" in her other ear. She tried to whack me with her free hand and almost fell off the stool.

"Wendy's my favorite aunt," she shouted down the tube.

The conversation progressed. I leaned against the pantry shelves, careful not to dislodge any jars of beans or tomato sauce. After a few minutes, Sara shouted a final "Love you, Mom!" into the receiver and set the earpiece back on its hook.

"I think we're alone now," she whispered to me, quoting our favorite song. "There doesn't seem to be anyone around."

"And the beating of your heart is the only sound," I finished the line, keeping time with my knuckle on a big can of cooking oil.

It was sunrise on the ranch and midmorning in New York. The whole day beckoned us.

"How about a big cowboy breakfast!" Sara poked my ribs. "Mom probably has her prune juice by her side. Or her martini!"

"I'm sure I heard her give us her blessings," she concluded with a crisp nod.

A knock at the kitchen door interrupted our repartee. Sara stayed in the pantry while I strode across the tile floor to open the door for the cowboy, who carried two buckets of milk; he set them on the drain board by the sink. I thanked him and he headed back out into the October dawn.

Sara emerged and stretched to slide the enamel milk pans from their shelf above the sink. She stood on her toes a second longer than necessary to make sure I admired her calves. She separated the four nested pans and divided the contents of the buckets among them.

"You're not going to invite him for breakfast?" she teased me. "He looks like he could play that old harmonica my mother dreads. I should have told her you call it a mouth organ out here! That would have knocked her off her Chippendale."

"Ah, well, back to business," she finished. "Bacon and eggs for us; real cream in our coffee. What's on tap for today?"

Since my own parents had moved out, I was faced with decisions like this; it also meant we had the house to ourselves. I thought for a moment. "Tacho and the cowboys will be down at the shipping corrals, their third day. The boys'll finish creosoting the corrals and Tacho's set to clean the scales. A zillion spiders get in and under them over the summer and we need to have them perfect when the buyers show up. He'll check the balance and lube the cantilevers all the way from the bar to the platform."

"It's work he likes. Sometimes there's a snake or two back there. He'll call them out."

"He's such a cool guy," Sara smiled. "With one or two words he can tell me so much. He loves this place like you do; you can tell by the way he smiles when you show him something new."

"His wife's great, too. She taught me how to cook those doves you guys shot. I picked out the pellets. My father would have been proud of me."

"Hang onto that recipe," I responded, slicing a few strips of bacon off the slab that hung in the pantry. The smoky aroma trailed me back into the kitchen.

"The desert is so-what's the right word-understated? Subtle?" Sara mused as she laid the bacon slices in the pan "To an Easterner it all looks the same at first. But you and Tacho see so much. I'm learning to see it, too."

"Well, Tacho and I were born here, so we had a head start. We had to learn those subtleties early. Otherwise we'd put our hands or feet on something prickly or poisonous or both."

I thought of Tacho's new wife, adapting to the ranch just as Sara was. "Sofia is new to this part of the desert; I think her family's from way down South, high country. She's still getting used to the heat. Tacho told me October's her favorite month."

"But his family's been here since this was part of Mexico; probably since it was part of Spain or even earlier, " I added. "Remember the Gadsden Purchase from our American Studies class? Gadsden makes our current occupant look like a saint!"

"I thought this was the day you weren't getting into politics," Sara humored me. "And where would your great-grandfather have found work without Gadsden's railroad? Building it is what brought him here—or so your family legend goes."

I didn't rise to her bait so she gave up teasing me and focused on the bacon. When the sizzle filled the kitchen, Sara pushed the strips to the edge of the pan, broke a few eggs into the grease and scrambled them with her fork. In a moment, breakfast was ready and we slid it onto plates and sat at the table. A chunk of bread and the coffee pot rested at our elbows.

"So that accounts for Tacho and the cowboys," Sara resumed her line of thought. "What's your plan?"

"I thought I'd show you my favorite picnic spot."

"The one where you took all your old girlfriends?" Sara wrinkled her nose.

"No!" I exclaimed. "This one I saved just for you!"

"Besides, they didn't like horses," I went on, "and this place you can only get to on a horse. Or hiking. And who would hike when they can ride?"

"You got me there," Sara laughed. "So what do we need to do before we head out?"

"I'll feed the calves and the pigs if you'll water the garden and pick a few tomatoes. Watch for snakes."

"No kidding," Sara widened her eyes at me. "I surprised two bullsnakes mating in the squash patch yesterday and they hissed at me just like rattlers. I thought your snakes were supposed to be hibernating by now!"

"Those two must not have read their job description," I smiled at her over my eggs. "I told them to test you! Don't worry, you'll know a rattler when you hear one; it's hardwired in our genes. People might mistake a locust for a rattlesnake but no one ever mistakes a rattler for a locust. Or the hissing of a bullsnake."

"Rattlers are special. You want to meet one, talk to Tacho; he's on a first-name basis."

"I'll pass." Sara wrinkled her nose again. She was cute and tan and I loved her. Even better, she loved me.

"Snakes eat rats…" I began, but Sara finished my sentence before I could,

"…and sixty rats eat as much as a calf so every sixty rats the snakes get puts a hundred bucks in my pocket! See, I'm learning ranch economics!" she laughed. "and all its externalities."

"It's your externalities I love," I smiled across the table. I finished my eggs, stood up, blew her a kiss, and grabbed my hat. "I'll be back at ten with the horses. There's tons of stuff for a picnic; be sure to fill four canteens. We can ride out right from here."

I reached for the doorknob.

"Hold on, horse man," Sara blocked my way. "This is a toll door. Pay the toll!"

I gave her a real kiss and it lingered, became a hug. She pressed her body to mine and I responded. She slid her fingers lightly along my neck and then let me go. "Feed your little piggies," she whispered. "I'll go check out those nice round ripe tomatoes; maybe I'll pick a cucumber, too, if it's hard enough."

"Cuke season ended in July!" I protested. "They're all pickled and in the pantry!"

Then I caught her jest. I blushed and slipped out the door.

Three hours later I came back with two horses saddled. Tacho's wife Sofia met me on our porch; in a hemp sling she carried a gallon of milk and a pint of cream, the glass jars wrapped in wet white linen.

"Hi Boss!" she greeted me. "Your *novia's* all set. You two are so lucky; when Tacho and I were going out, my *tías* followed us everywhere. And his grandmother, too."

She lowered her voice and narrowed her eyes at me, her dark face serious, "You treat her right, now! I can call my *tías* anytime and they'll camp out right here on your porch! You won't be able to steal a kiss 'til you're married!"

Sofia's smile returned. "She showed me her ring. It's just right. Don't let her get away!"

"Who've you got for horses?" she changed the subject, satisfied that Sara was well protected for the moment.

I returned her smile. "Mitch and Caroline. They don't bite either."

"No horse would dare bite me!" Sofia shifted her sling and skipped by me to scratch the big mare's forehead with her knuckles and plant a kiss on her nose. "They know I bite back!"

"I'll remember that," I looped the two sets of reins around the porch post. "We'll be back by four. Take some tomatoes if you like. We can get frost any night now."

“OK, thanks,” Sofia was already headed down the path. “I hope so!” she concluded. “My bees are ready to shut down for the winter; they’re not used to this heat. Thick air at this altitude!”

I left Sofia to her garden and turned back toward my house. I looped our horses’ reins over the porch rail and rapped at the screen door to the kitchen. Sara had our picnic ready in another hemp sling. She filled four canteens and we split the load, hanging the water off either side of our pommels. I lashed the hemp bag behind the saddle where it would avoid catching twigs as we rode.

Despite my warning to Sofia about the coming frost, the day was warm. We set out in our shirtsleeves, up from Headquarters Pasture onto National Forest land. Tall grass left from the summer rains tickled our stirrups and the horses pulled the grain from the stalks alongside the trail. I made half an effort to keep Mitch focused, but we were in no hurry. He sensed he would see few cattle today, and drive none.

Above Headquarters the Cancione foothills sprouted like coral reefs above the high desert. We wound our way up a dry streambed in the narrowing valley floor. I pointed out to Sara the demarcation between blue oaks and white oaks, right at 5,000 feet; and then manzanita and juniper as the valley narrowed even further and the trail steepened. Summer rains had ended a few weeks back, about the time Sara arrived; the grass on the south face of the foothills was already fading, but the north slopes still rippled green as the sea. Bright ruby fruit swelled on the prickly pears and ocatilla spikes danced on the sunny hillsides.

Before long, the dry streambed we followed dampened where willows overhung its banks, and soon seeps of water began to dot its shady side. The sound of water flowing far ahead reached first our horses' ears, and then ours; rounding a bend, we came upon a trickle, which in a few hundred yards grew to a spring-fed freshet.

At last we arrived at our destination. The streambed, which had by this point narrowed to only a few yards wide, suddenly opened into a wide basin of smooth flat granite bordered by tall cottonwood trees. The stream meandered through the granite, seeking its course and tumbling over a series of little waterfalls into a string of still pools.

The waterfalls generated the sound we had heard way downstream.

At the top of the basin, where rivulets from two side canyons fed the stream, the granite tabletop widened to fifty feet or so. An old windmill tower rose from the junction, silhouetted against the mountainside. The tower was rusted and the old mill was gap-toothed but it still worked, plunging its sucker rod into the crack in the granite between the canyons, chugging water from a rusty pipe onto the stone tank.

"Here we are!" I called to Sara.

"What an amazing place!" she exclaimed, reining Caroline in beside me and standing up in her stirrups to get a better view. "How on earth did that windmill get here?"

"The CCC hauled it in piece-by-piece back in the thirties. They built all these trails, all over the Southwest. Deer and wild horses were here, but almost no one hiked or rode; that's when the whole National Forest system got started. Jobs in the Depression. My grandparents were here at Headquarters, but the mountains were wild. Grandfather used to tell stories about the CCC workers. They camped out at the ranch and worked for years all over the mountains. My grandmother got a little stipend from the Government to cook for them."

"You'd of thought they would be a rough lot but she said they were polite as could be. Artists and engineers and surveyors; all kinds of men. They'd lost their jobs back East."

"What became of them?" Sara wondered.

"The war."

"Then you were born out here, and I was born in New York, and look at us now! And that old wind-mill is still turning. Do the cattle come to drink?"

"No, it's like stairs up above; cows can't come down stairs. And cows will almost never walk uphill to water. So you'll see deer and *chulus* and they say there's a few wild horses left, but I've never seen one. It's all here just to be beautiful. For you."

"I love it!" she leaned over to whisper in my ear. Caroline sidled closer to Mitch so Sara could keep her balance.

"This land will never be touched. It's all yours. Let's eat!" I nudged her back into her saddle and then swung off Mitch. I was hungry; breakfast seemed a week ago.

"It's not a real picnic without flowers!" Sara slid down from her saddle. "I'll find us a cozy place to eat. You go up around the bend and pick me a bouquet. Red and blue and white. No yellow! I'll tie the horses in the shade and loosen their cinches."

I rolled my eyes. I was hungry. But she was right; there'd be a ton of flowers in the damp dappled light up one of the canyons above the windmill. I headed out.

"Watch out for snakes!" Sara mimicked me. I waved my hat and clambered upstream.

I found thistle poppies, Shasta daisies, penstamon and a bright red deer's tongue for the center of the bouquet. I wrapped the stems in a smooth yucca leaf and turned the edges under so nothing was sharp. "Not bad," I thought. "Maybe she'll pick something like this for her bridal bouquet." I headed back downstream.

Past the windmill and the waterfalls and pools, I caught sight of the horses tied to a cottonwood near the bottom of the basin. I didn't see Sara until I almost tripped over her.

Sara had shed her clothes and was sitting motionless on the warm granite, her legs primly crossed and her arms folded over her breasts.

"Camouflage!" she yipped when I startled back a step. "You told me that's the secret of the desert, and it works!"

I laughed out loud. "You're so right! But your not prickly or poisonous, I hope!" I knelt down and presented her the bouquet. "For you, my alabaster goddess!"

"You're so gallant." She extended one hand and took the bouquet, her other arm still draped coyly across her nipples. She smiled up at me for a heartbeat. "I guess I'd better get some water for these posies."

Sara stood and stretched and tiptoed up toward the waterfall. She looked over one shoulder, holding the bouquet out for balance. "I'll be right back!"

The only sounds were the windmill and the water. My stomach no longer clamored for my attention. In a moment she returned, the flower stems wrapped in a white cloth. She looked down at me with an appraising eye. "Your lunch is in the shade, " she winked at me. "But it's so nice here in the sun. I see you got so hot you were forced to shed your garments, sir. Why don't we take a little time before we picnic?"

Afterwards she pulled me into the pool. The water was like ice, but the day was dry and soon we were too. We rested on the clean white granite and enjoyed our lunch. The afternoon waned. As the sun lengthened to the west, the old windmill gleamed red against the mountain.

Sara said yes.

We took our time going home. After supper Sara called her father; he was reading and happy to hear from her.

Sara handed me the receiver and stepped off the stool. She retreated to the kitchen to run water on our dishes. I spoke with her father for a few moments.

"Thank you, sir," I said into the tube, my voice echoing back through the receiver as I listened to his reply.

"I certainly will." I answered him. "I think my parents will be happy too. Sara and I be back East for Thanksgiving and I'll bring you some of that honey she raves about."

"Oh, and this is a party line," I reminded him. "So you should tell all your friends and neighbors our good news, too."

GOOD NEIGHBOR

The trail curled around the scrub juniper and opened into the pasture. I could see my neighbor Tom at the upper fence line, bending to his work. His Jeep was in the shade of the big oak by the corner.

Sheriff Gants' panel truck squatted a few hundred feet east along the fence. As I drove into the pasture, I saw the lawman picking his way up toward Tom, peering at the ground.

It was April and wildflowers carpeted the pasture. The California Poppies shone so orange I almost had to squint, or at least focus on the deer's tongue and dusty purple penstamon where the soil was thin.

Every few years the pasture dressed up like this. It was as though Goya shook out his paintbrush on the desert, except a hundred times brighter under the cobalt sky. Out in the center of the pasture, where the flowers got the best sun and drainage, the track all but disappeared. I followed it more by feel than by sight.

When I got within a couple of hundred feet of the fence, Gants looked up from his task and waved for me to stop. Right in the sun. The steering wheel would be hotter than the hinges of hell in twenty minutes, but I knew what he had in mind, so I killed the engine and stepped out, knee deep in flowers.

Gants was sweating. He took off his white Stetson and wiped his brow with his sleeve. I stayed on the track and waited for him by the gate.

"They didn't use the gate," he said. "Parked here and walked up to where Tom's at so they could sit under the tree and watch the water.'

"When the cattle came in at sundown they picked the one they wanted and shot it from there. It looks like they dragged it up out of the canyon with their truck and skinned it by the tree. They cut the fence right where Tom's at. It must've been dark by the time they got done but they didn't use their lights on the way out."

"I got a little paint off the fencepost and some plaster from the tracks."

Tom hadn't looked up, although he was working less than fifty feet up the fence line. Bees buzzed in the flowers and I could see he was concentrating on the barbed wire, fence staples clenched in his teeth as he stretched the splice and held it with his knee against the post. It was meticulous work and if you slipped, the best that could happen was stitches in your hand. We waited until he had the wire set and then walked up the line.

Tom took the couple of staples from between his teeth and nodded to me. "Thanks for coming. There's the hide." He hung his yellow fencing pliers on the top strand and we walked up into the oak shade. The hide crumpled dark against the tree. The brand had been cut out of the withers, just as he had told Gants and me on the phone.

"It's probably yours, because they cut the fence down by the water, too. You'd of thought they'd have enough sense to shoot one on this side, but no. I bagged up the gut." He looked expectantly at me. I should have offered to take it and bury it right then, but I held my peace.

Gants pointed to the tracks in the dust under the oak tree. "I figure there were three of them," he said. "One kid wearing sneakers—I took a cast—and a couple of men in work boots. There's good tracks down by the water. The stock haven't been back; they're probably spooked. Yours are probably still on the other side, even though they cut the fence. I don't think they'd come through where the dead one's been dragged."

Tom and I exchanged glances and the corner of his mouth twitched so softly that Gants wouldn't have caught it. Gants wore work boots too. We'd seen him once on a horse and it was not pretty.

Tom and I went over to the hide and without asking Gants we shook it out in the shade. We squatted on our heels and checked the markings. Most of the flies clustered around the head and skull. No horns, but we could see the scars from last spring: yearling heifer, grade. "My heifers are mostly up the mountain already," Tom said. He was right, and I knew I'd get to take the guts back and bury them, and said as much.

We set for a few more minutes, the dark shade surrounded by the riot of color. I looked down the pasture. Tom got up and took his big canvas canteen off the front of his Jeep and offered me a long draught. The water was cold and good. Gants fidgeted.

"OK, then." I said. "I'll fix the fence down by the trough." I looked back to the sheriff. "You got castings of the tire tracks by the gate? I'd like to come up through so I don't have to lug the wire through the brush. It's early for snakes but I'd just as soon get as close as I can. I'll come in town as soon as we get the fences fixed and fill out the paperwork."

"Give me ten more minutes." He said. "Damn stuff dries so fast in the sun, it gets brittle and I have to keep wetting it down while I pour." He headed back to his truck in the sun.

Tom and I squatted in the shade until he was done and gone and then I put my Jeep next to Tom's, got my hammer, and we finished his fence together so he could get home for dinner by noon.

POWDER KEG

On his thirteenth birthday our son Linnaeus announced he would no longer eat venison, nor would he hunt deer.

His decision sidetracked a family tradition that went back four generations, but it created an opportunity for his sister Andrea. She was eleven at the time. Before we finished Linnaeus' birthday, cake, Andrea had affirmed her gusto for both eating and hunting deer, and staked her claim to any potential deer rifle and set of buckhorns that Linnaeus' future might have held.

I raised my eyebrows and opened my mouth to protest, but Sara nudged me under the table with her foot so I held my tongue. She addressed Andrea, "Great, next November, right after roundup's over, Dad will take you up the mountain. We'll need two deer in the freezer but I wouldn't shoot Bambi's mama, so if Linnaeus is out, that leaves you!"

Thus, the decision was made without a word from me.

Throughout fall roundup the following November, Andrea reminded me of the decision. Deer season started on the Saturday after we shipped calves, the day we returned all the cattle to their pastures. The following day, a month before Andrea's twelfth birthday, she and I cleaned two rifles. We set our scopes, punching tight patterns on targets set in the sandy bank of the arroyo below Headquarters.

We cleaned our rifles again and were set to hunt.

Before dawn on Monday morning, Sara fixed us a big breakfast, gave Andrea her bright orange down-filled vest, and packed lunches.

Up the mountain we went. That day, Linnaeus rode the school bus alone.

It felt strange for Andrea and me to walk trails we usually rode, but it was part of the tradition. As my father had me, I taught Andrea to walk uphill with the wind in her face, placing and lifting her feet with care, a cartridge in her rifle's chamber. She had memorized and could recite the rules of gunmanship as quickly as poets quote Yeats. She was excited to shoot her first buck.

November was bleak and cold in the high desert. We hiked up through the oaks and junipers and into the pines. The forest held its breath, as ours grew labored and steamed into the thinning air. I pointed out grottoes where deer had yarded-up through the windy night and left their droppings; smooth bark where bucks had rubbed the velvet from their antlers.

We crossed and followed some deer tracks but saw no white tails flash.

By midmorning, we had reached the ridge crest and we worked our way along it into the wind. By noon, Andrea was tired of walking and my toes were ice cubes. We decided to yard up too and rest.

West of the ridge, we found a spring and a nearby fire pit. This made a good base; we agreed that after we ate we'd find a deer trail, take a stand upwind, and try waiting rather than stalking.

Andrea gathered dry wood and built a small fire in the pit. We brought forth our lunches. In Andrea's pack, in addition to her lunch, she found a sealed envelope from her mother. She opened and read its contents, raised her eyebrows and without sharing tucked it into her pocket.

We lingered over lunch and tarried by the fire. The thought of climbing a fir tree to sit motionless in the biting wind at the top of the ridge appealed less and less as the time passed.

The fire blazed. "Maybe we'll have better luck tomorrow?" I suggested. "And we always have the hike down. Maybe the wind will shift and we'll see something," I added.

"That could mean shooting toward the ranch," Andrea noted.

"True enough." I mused. I tried a new tack, "Hunting's different from target shooting, isn't it?'

"I hunt rabbits," Andrea frowned at me. "They're easy; we just stand in the back of the Jeep and pop them. Why all this drama with deer? Why not just drive up to the top where we know they hang out and pop them like we do rabbits? They eat grass too! They're just big rats."

"Then we wouldn't have to drag the carcass down the mountain either; we could just throw it in the Jeep."

I chuckled. "Well, it's a ritual," I began. "Deer are big game; nobody stuffs and mounts jackrabbits. Unless it's a joke, like the jackalope in the Frontier Hotel lobby."

"That's so lame, Dad," was her retort.

"I wish I was old enough to hunt deer alone. And drive. That way I could come up in the Jeep and bring one back, easy."

It was hard to argue with her logic. She's noticed the jackalope over the bar in the hotel the first time she'd been there, when she was about three years old. Even then she thought it was lame.

"Well, like I said, it's a ritual. Deer hunting's when fathers, and, um, their kids, get to go off together for some quality time," I ventured, grateful I'd caught myself before I said "their sons."

Andrea wasn't fooled. She poked at the fire and burned the wax paper from her sandwich. She stood up and stretched and paced around the fire pit, looking thoughtful. I watched her, amazed how tall she had grown, almost a woman, wondering where the years had gone since my little girl was born.

After a moment, Andrea seemed to come to some sort of resolution. She squatted by the fire again. "Speaking of rituals," she picked up my theme, "Was Miss Lynch a racist when you had her?"

Her question took me aback. Miss Lynch was the principal at Andrea and Linnaeus' school, a three-room whitewashed adobe structure at the crossroads in the valley below the ranch. She was already the principal twenty years earlier when I graduated from eighth grade; she seemed ancient then, but she was probably all of forty, which made her about sixty by now. In addition to serving as Principal, she taught sixth through eighth grades, all in the same room.

I knew Miss Lynch pretty well and my first impulse was to deny the racism charge. But I realized that Andrea had asked a sincere question; now she looked straight at me, waiting for a sincere answer. She was testing me; maybe testing herself, too.

I rolled her question around in my mind. I remembered a parenting tactic Sara often used, "That's an interesting question, " I began. "Why do you ask?"

"Give me a break, Dad, there's nobody listening. You can tell the truth."

Again, her passion surprised me. I thought back to my three years in Miss Lynch's classroom. She'd been strict, but fair, at least to me. I racked my brain for a recollection of how she had treated my classmates who were Indian or Mexican or Black. Memories nibbled at the edge of my conscience and then bit hard. I pondered the best way to parse my reply to Andrea.

My daughter raised her eyebrows as she watched me think. She suddenly looked a lot like her mother, and I wondered what Sara had written in her letter.

Andrea was growing up; this was her first year in Miss Lynch's classroom and she had two more to anticipate. Whatever I said would affect those years. I resolved to answer her as truthfully as I could.

"Well, " I began, "most White people say or do things sometimes that could be seen as racist from a certain point of view."

"Like the point of view of anyone who isn't White?" Andrea asked pointedly.

Another hard question.

I sighed. The fire had died down and I got another couple of pine branches and stirred them in before I answered. Their cones flared hot. Andrea waited patiently. She had nowhere else she wanted to be.

"Back to your first question, I guess I'd say yes," I finally offered. "And your second question's an affirmative, too."

Andrea relaxed and smiled grimly. Now it was my turn to ask her a question and expect a serious answer, "What got you thinking so much about racism all of a sudden?"

Andrea decided she could level with me. This was an adult conversation and so far I had treated her like an adult. "Last week, Miss Lynch got on Anita's case for something or other, you know how the old bat gets," she began.

I nodded.

"So, anyway, Anita usually just listens and doodles on the back of her hand. But this time she totally lost it. She shouted at Miss Lynch that she was sick and tired of her picking on her because she was Mexican. And then she called her a racist, right to her face, right there in class."

"Wow," I replied. "That's not like Anita. She's so laid back; I've never seen her lose it like that."

"Me neither," Andrea nodded. "That's why I've been stressing about it, ever since it happened. I actually asked her about it on the bus, but she blew me off. She told me to ask her Dad and then she changed the subject, started talking about horses, you know how she is. But I didn't want to ask Mr. Lopez; he's so, well, you know, so big!"

"Not that he's not a great guy," she hastened to add.

I nodded and poked the fire. I thought of the times over the years I'd watched Tacho deal with racism, sometimes overt, more often just implied. He'd gone to school on the west side of town, so he'd never had Miss Lynch as his teacher. But he knew her, as did all the parents.

I wondered how Tacho might respond to Andrea's questions but I knew she'd never ask him. It was up to me.

"After Anita called her a racist, what did Miss Lynch say?" I asked.

"That's when it got way weird," Andrea replied. "Generally, Miss Lynch has an answer for everything, she just steps back with this big attitude and she tells you. That's that. She's a teacher." Andrea wrinkled her nose as if she had smelled something dead.

"But last week she freaked! She gabbed Anita by the hair and slapped her face and shouted at her, something like, 'Don't you ever speak to me like that again!' And Anita started to cry, real quiet, but we could all hear her, and Miss Lynch let go of her hair and went over to the water fountain and brought her back a cup of water and put it on her desk. Real nice all of a sudden. Weird."

"Then she looked at the rest of us and told us to mind our own business and get back to work. Like we were the problem, not her."

"So how did the other kids react?" I asked. "What about Linnaeus? He's in Anita's class, right?"

Andrea twisted her mouth dismissively. "Linnaeus wouldn't fight a gila monster if it was chewing on his pecker!" she retorted.

"Andrea! He's your brother! You shouldn't use language like that about anyone, especially your brother!"

She rolled her eyes. "Come on, Dad, I've heard you use that expression a hundred times; where do you think I learned it?"

I let it go for the moment. I wanted to known more about the scene in the classroom. "Did anyone say anything?"

"No, and that's what really makes me sad. Anita just sat there and sniffled until the end of class and then she went and locked herself in the stall in the girl's room. She didn't touch the water Miss Lynch brought her."

"A couple of us went into the girl's room during recess and tried to get her to come out but she wouldn't; she wouldn't even answer us. So after a while we got onto something else. When she came out, she was her regular self; I didn't say anything about it 'til we were almost home, and it was just her and Linnaeus and her little brother and me left on the bus. Nico didn't see it;

he's in fifth grade, and I don't know if he even knows what happened."

"Next day, it was like everything was cool again. But Daddy, it's really got me down, I don't know what I should do!" Andrea's eyes suddenly filled with tears and I moved around the fire and held her; she sobbed against my chest.

My eyes filled with tears too, for my daughter, for her friend, for Tacho and his family. I held Andrea for a few moments and she composed herself. I gave her my handkerchief and she wiped her face. "I'm sorry," she began.

"Don't!" I reassured her. "You've got every right to be upset, angry, whatever! No matter what Anita said, Miss Lynch doesn't have the right to pull her hair and slap her! I'll take care of this!"

"No, Dad, don't say anything; Miss Lynch would kill me! I've got to go back in there every day; we all do."

I sighed. I felt drained, helpless; but, at the same time thankful that this secret, hidden for a generation, was finally out in the open. I wished Andrea and I could stay snuggled in this warm pocket on the hip of the mountain we loved. But the real world was down in the valley.

I gathered my strength. "We're a family, all of us on the ranch," I began. "And we need to do something. The fact that Miss Lynch snapped shows that Anita hit the nail on the head. Miss Lynch is a racist; we all sensed that when we were in school, too, but no one ever had the guts to confront her. And now, you and Anita and your friends are still having to deal with her."

"School shouldn't be like that. If there's anywhere in the world kids should feel safe, it's at school."

Andrea nodded, but I could tell she wasn't convinced yet. I felt like I had leapt into a bottomless pit, but I pressed on.

"I can see you feel trapped, sweetheart. We did too; we couldn't wait to get to high school, all of us—Black, White, whatever color we were. We were all ashamed but we didn't talk about it, except, maybe some of the Black kids did; but they didn't bring us White kids in. They just endured. Or most of them did."

My conscience pricked me again. I thought about my Black and Mexican classmates. Some of them still lived in the area, but most of them had left; joined the Army or moved to town or just disappeared. I wondered why I'd never thought of them before now. So much could have been said, but never was. Maybe Andrea's generation could start anew.

I thumped my gloved fist into my palm. "You and Anita don't have to take this all over again. It's wrong. It's hateful. Mom and I love you, Linnaeus loves you, and Anita's family loves her. You're both stronger than we ever were, and we've got to believe it's because our families love each other and we love our kids. Together we'll figure this out."

"What if Tacho and I went in and confronted Miss Lynch?" I wondered out loud. "Maybe with your Mom and Sofia and some other parents?"

"Anita would die," Andrea protested. "I bet she didn't even tell her parents. They're so, like, traditional? I mean, they speak Spanish at home, like all the Mexican kids do. And the Black kids hang together, and Linnaeus and I, we just do our thing most of the time, too."

"Don't underestimate Tacho and Sofia," I disagreed. "They're not that traditional. She's got a degree in biology and he's one of the smartest men I've ever met. Just plain smart. You can bet they know Miss Lynch is a racist, and maybe they're waiting for us to wake up. Maybe you're the one who can break out of all this, for all the kids."

"I don't think so, Dad."

"Okay, then suppose we don't do anything. Where does that leave you and the rest of the kids? We'd be just as bad as she is. Racism's like an infection that festers more if you cover it up. We need to do something."

Andrea finally nodded, more resigned than relieved. I felt drained.

"So, shall we hunt some more?" she asked tentatively. "I'm sorry to lay this all on you, Dad. I know you love me; I love you and Mom and Linnaeus, even when he's a creep. Which is most of the time," she rolled her eyes.

"But seriously, Dad, I am glad I told you, 'cause I didn't know what I should do. I still don't, but at least I know you don't either."

"Racism sucks, doesn't it?" she concluded.

"Yeah. But we are going to do something. Let's head down the mountain, maybe we'll get lucky and some deer will trip and break its leg right in front of us."

"Close." But Andrea smiled up at me, and I knew we had cleared one hurdle. She picked up her gun and carefully wiped a few leaves from the barrel. She checked the chamber and the safety and stepped carefully up the little trail toward the ridge. I kicked the fire apart in the pit, covered the coals and ashes with a few flat rocks. I checked my gun and followed her up to the ridge.

We retraced our steps along the ridgeline, the wind at our backs now. It seemed warmer; the western sun silhouetted Andrea as she picked her way carefully along the trail, cradling her rifle so it always pointed down and aside, easy to protect even if she stumbled. I felt a multitude of pride in her. And I pondered our next step.

When we reached the flats above Headquarters, I called to her to hold up a second; she turned and looked back questioningly.

"You hear something? A deer?"

"No, I wish!" I replied. "I just wanted to run something by you before we get home; ask your advice like you asked mine when we were up on top."

"Okay."

"Imagine you were me: whatever power I might have, you have. If you could see a way through this situation with Miss Lynch, what would it look like?'

Andrea propped her rifle in the cleft of a dead mesquite by the gate into Headquarters pasture, pointed up and away from Headquarters and from the two of us. She took off her Day-Glo gloves and cap and ran her fingers through her hair, thinking about my question.

Finally she spoke, picking her words with care: "Okay, you guys have the power to vote, and, you elect the school board, and, they hire Miss Lynch. Right?

"Basically, yes."

"Who's on the school board?" she asked. "Are there any Mexicans or Indians or Blacks? They'd understand what happened, or at least they might believe it actually did happen. And that it happens all the time, maybe not with the hair pulling and slapping, but with the grades Anita gets and the way Miss Lynch follows her and the other kids around, as if they're going to steal something or whatever."

I pictured the school board in my mind. "No luck there," I finally concluded. "They're good people, but they're all White. You know them: there's Kenny's dad and Amanda's big sister and Mr. Angus. He's been on the school board since I was there; his son Red runs the ranch in the La Garita's, where we go for the barbecue at election time. Red was in my class when I was in your school."

"Mr. Angus!" Anita exclaimed. "I know him! He's this real old guy, wrinkled as all get out, older than Grandpa. He came in to my class last year and did this experiment with us!"

"He's been on the school board since you were there?" She knit her brow, thinking, scheming. It was a look I'd seen when she and Linnaeus were plotting something. "Yeah," she said slowly, nodding her head. "He's our guy."

"What makes you say that?" I was curious now; old man Angus had always been an enigma to me, to all of us. I tried to remember if he'd ever come into the classroom when we were in school.

Andrea picked up her story: "He came in during the last week of school, when everybody's itchy, and sat right on Miss Sawyer's desk. He had this neat old cane, it was made of real dark wood and had some kind of bone, no, antlers, I think, for a handle. Not whitetail antlers, some other kind, maybe some African deer."

"Anyway, he came in and just sat on the edge of her desk, kind of tapping the handle of his cane with his fingernails until everyone got real quiet. Spooky, but cool. Like he was waiting for us to come to him."

"Then he looked at us real close and he said, 'Some of you have brown eyes, and some of you have blue eyes.'"

"'Like, duh', I thought at the time, but then he stood up and hobbled right over to me and said, 'You, little lady, you have blue eyes, you stand in that corner.' He pointed with the cane and it was kind of like the corner glowed. Spooky, but cool. I looked at Miss Sawyer and she nodded, so I did like he said."

"He went down one row and up the next and everyone who had blue eyes, he made us stand in the corner. Maybe ten of us out of thirty or so. Including Miss Sawyer."

Andrea smiled at her memory. "So we're standing in the corner, kind of fidgeting around, and he goes and sets back on the side of her desk. He says to the kids who are left, 'OK, brown eyes, you're the majority here. You get to rule this classroom. Those blue-eyes, they're your servants. They have to do anything you tell them to do. I'm the law; I'll make sure they do it. Or else!' He whacked the desk with his cane and scared the, you know, out of us."

"That's quite a story, "I said. "And Miss Sawyer let him do this?"

"Oh, yeah! She told us all about it after he left. It's from some book. But it really worked, Dad! We didn't need the book! We watched what happened next!"

"So tell me," I prodded her.

She needed no encouragement. Her face lit up, and for the first time since we left the mountaintop I saw her old spunk. "At first the brown eyes were cool; they just asked us to bring them a cup of water or sharpen their pencil and stuff like that. But then Wizzy, you know, Jasmine's little sister, she got it—she saw that she could demand anything—and she went up to

Carl, and she made him take off his shirt and give it to her."

"Miss Sawyer just let it happen!" Andrea threw her arms in the air, the Day-Glow gloves adding emphasis.

"And then Casey, that creepy kid from across the draw, he came up and told me I had to give him my shirt! Just because he had brown eyes and mine were blue!"

Andrea grew more pensive. "But Miss Sawyer stopped him, said that was against the rules, and Mr. Angus nodded, so Casey backed down."

She nodded and continued her story: "But then Mr. Angus said to all of us with the blue eyes: 'What if Miss Sawyer or I wasn't here just now? What if the brown eyes could take your shirt right off your back—even from a woman—suppose they had the power to do that? After all, they're the majority: if they decided they didn't like the color of your eyes, they could force you blue eyes to do whatever they want!'"

"So then he pointed his cane at the brown eyes kids and he asked them what they would take, supposing they could take anything they wanted, 'cause they were the majority, and he got some really scary answers."

"He listed some of them on the board. Then he read us something from this old book. Some guy wrote it back when Washington or Lincoln or somebody was President, and Mr. Angus had the real book."

"What did it say?" I pressed her.

"Something about tyranny. He asked us if we knew what a tyrant was, and Wizzy, she's way smart, you know, she said it was like that big dinosaur, T-Rex? A bad king?"

"Um-hum. And what happened next?" I asked her.

"That was it. He took his book and his cane and left. But right before he hobbled out of the room, he turned around, and he pointed that cane at us again, and he said, real soft to us, so we could just barely hear it: 'You blue eyes, you remember today. Remember what it felt like for you to be powerless, even though you didn't do anything to deserve it, when you have power.'"

"Afterwards we talked about it. Miss Sawyer made it part of her lesson for a couple of days. Then school was out for the summer."

"What were you studying?

Andrea rolled her eyes. "Who knows? Some war. That's not the point, Dad, the point is, that old guy would know what Anita felt like. It was like Anita was one of us blue eyes, and old Miss Lynch, she was like that idiot Casey. He'd understand! And he's on the school board!"

"But Anita has brown eyes," I protested.

"Dad, you are so clueless! It's not about eye color! 'Nita wasn't even in the room! She was already up in Miss Lynch's class. It's about power! It's about racism! Judging people by the way they look. Jeez, I don't believe how dumb you can be!" She shook her head and laughed, but then she stepped over and gave me a hug.

"I love you, Dad. At least you listen, even if you don't hear too good."

"Too well." I murmured into her hair. "I hear what you're saying, sweetheart. Old Angus might get it. It's worth a try."

"But you and Anita need to get on the same page," I told her. "Tell her you talked to me. Tell her I understand, that I'll help. Convince her the way you convinced me."

"Once you've shown her you care—and I know you do—you'll win back her trust, then you and she need to sit down with Tacho and Sofia and your mother and me, and talk the whole thing through. Linnaeus needs to be there, too, and Nico."

I gave Andrea a tight hug. "If you get Anita's okay we'll get everyone for supper on Friday; Mom and Sofia like to do that anyway. It's cold and they'll make a stew. If it's okay with you, I'll talk to Mom, and tell her the whole story, including the blue eyes-brown eyes part. Then, at dinner on Friday, you and Anita tell your story."

"Tacho and Sofia will listen, trust me. I won't say anything to either of them before we all get together. You've got the power this time, like Mr. Angus said. Use it for good."

Andrea gave me a final squeeze and slipped back by the mesquite tree. "Yeah!" she nodded firmly. "This is something I can do." She picked up her rifle and ejected the cartridge from the chamber, slipped it in her pocket. She thumbed the clip release and dropped it down into her hand and pocketed it, too: the gun was empty. I did the same with mine before we set the guns over the fence and climbed through into Headquarters Pasture.

We were just coming around the house when the school bus rattled up the driveway and deposited Linnaeus, Anita and Nico by the cattleguard. Tacho's kids waved to us and ran up the path to their house; Linnaeus cat-walked across the rails and sauntered toward us.

"Where's your buck, hotshot?" he shouted to Andrea.

"I already ate it all!" she hollered back.

We three walked up the path to our home. Andrea and I put our rifles in the office and joined Linnaeus and Sara in the kitchen. Sara had honey and butter sandwiches and hot chocolate for us. We snacked, and after a bit our two children headed off to the barn to feed their stock.

"So, any deer, dear?" Sara asked when they were gone.

"Not the kind we were hunting," I smiled "The other kind, though, lots." I gave her a quick outline of our day.

Our families got together for supper the next Friday.

Andrea waited a few more Novembers to get her first buck, but at the end of December of that year, Miss Lynch unexpectedly took early retirement.

The school board expressed their gratitude for her many years of service and gave her a plaque.

In January, they named Miss Sawyer principal and moved her up to Andrea's and Anita's room. For grades three through five they hired a new teacher right out of the

University, a smart young Mexican woman who'd grown up on Red's ranch and had come home to visit her parents for the holiday.

"What good fortune!" all the parents exclaimed at the New Year's Day welcome party the school board hosted for the new teacher.

Old man Angus just clicked his antler cane and nodded.

LION HOUND

The old Navajo rug, a bit threadbare but still beautiful, lay on the wide board floor in the ranch living room; upon the rug lay King, the lion hound, and our daughter, Andrea.

King was fourteen years old and Andrea was nine. They were best friends.

Andrea smoothed the wrinkles on King's forehead and scratched behind his ears. She whispered to him and from time to time he groaned with pleasure and sighed deeply in response to her ministrations.

We knew King could not live too much longer, but he felt no pain this night. King had lived ten years longer than I once feared. The sight of the two of them on that rug always brought me joy.

Three weeks before Andrea was born, a mountain lion killed a yearling heifer high in Lookout Pasture. A deer hunter found the carcass by Cedar Spring and came by Headquarters to knock on our door that November evening. He hadn't recognized the brand, but we were the closest ranch: he knew the right thing to do.

We knew this hunter. Good men and women visited us at Headquarters at the start of deer season to alert us of their presence. This man had brought us a liver and heart two years back.

He stood in the dooryard at dusk, dressed in his red-and-black-checked wool jacket and hat, earflaps turned down. Sara, eight months pregnant, invited him in and offered him a cup of coffee. Her beef stew simmered on the stove.

That November was unusually cold, and we respected the fact that the hunter had gone out of his way. He sat and rested at the kitchen table with Sara, our son Linnaeus babbling in his nearby swing, while I walked to Tacho's house to invite him to join us.

When we were all together, the hunter described what he had discovered by the spring, "Your cow was cleaned out like she'd been field dressed," he began. "One hindquarter eaten from the inside, the bones picked and the skin all shriveled up, hard as cold iron."

"The rest of the carcass was chewed on some—big teeth marks—but it was all frozen solid. She'd been drug downhill a ways and it looked like whatever killed her had set to bury the carcass, because there were scratch marks all around; but it was too cold to dig. That got me thinking it was a lion. I climbed up above the spring a ways along the track, maybe a hundred feet or so, but then it hit me that if this was a lion's doing, I didn't want to hang around."

"So I hiked out and came by to tell you."

"How much would a cow like that weigh?" he asked. "It must have been a strong lion to drag a big cow that way!"

It was not a tactful time to explain to him the difference between a heifer and a cow, so I just answered his question, "Better than a thousand pounds. She was last year's calf; we put them on the mountain in the fall and leave them to grow."

"The lion will drag her prey downhill to water so she can come and go at will. You were smart not to linger. You can bet she knew you were there, although they won't often come after a human."

Sara poured Tacho a cup of coffee and set the pitcher of cream at his elbow. She settled into her rocking chair.

"Note he blames this on a woman," Sara finished my reply to the hunter. "In this case, he's right, much as I hate to admit it. It's the female lions who hunt."

The hunter raised his bushy eyebrows. "What are you going to do?" he asked. "Can I help?"

"Tacho and I'll take a ride up there tomorrow and look it over," I mused. "Lions have their territory, she won't be far from Cedar Spring; and other lions will give that area a wide berth."

"If she's killed that heifer she'll probably go after more; they only go after beef when something's slowed them down and they can't get a deer. Lions are your competition, you know: deer are their natural prey."

Sara got up and filled our guest's coffee, offering him a plate of donut holes. I gave her my "don't get started" look. It was getting dark out and we didn't want this guy for dinner, helpful as he was.

The hunter took a donut hole and dipped it in his coffee. "Well, I'm sorry for your loss. On the other point, I don't mind a few lions: they keep our deer herd healthy. They harvest the weak ones."

"But I knew when I saw that beef that this lion had to go."

I winced; Sara gave him a sweet smile, leaned across the table and took a donut hole. She offered me one but I declined.

Tacho sat back and watched the show. He knew I considered deer competition for the feed our heifers deserved: we paid to lease that pasture. He knew the "our deer" comment would drive me nuts.

"You need help?" the hunter asked again, eager to be part of a new hunt.

"Thanks for your offer," Tacho came to my defense. "But the fewer of us who go up after a lion, the safer. It's a quick hunt but plenty can go wrong. Those cats are smart and tricky and they've got big teeth. If this one's injured, she's even more dangerous."

"You don't want to be there when she trees," he smiled at the hunter. "I don't particularly want to be there either, but I can't get out of it." Tacho laughed and motioned toward me with his chin. "Boss says so."

"OK, then," the hunter let it go. I felt relieved and silently thanked Tacho with my eyes. Sara would tease me all night, but not Tacho.

The hunter finished his coffee and stood up. He had a long drive ahead of him and no deer on his fender. If Cedar Spring was his stand, hunting season was over for him, and he knew it. "Here's my number," he handed me a slip of paper. "I'd of left it on the door if you were out."

"Good luck to you," he picked up his red flannel hat, "and to you, ma'am. Thanks for the coffee. I'll be on my way."

Dark came early in late November. Tacho and I walked the hunter to his car, a beat-up old Ford. "This is my hunting car," he said, almost apologetically. "It goes anywhere; if the road's too steep I back it up the slope. Reverse is lower than first. I hate to drag my big bucks any further than I have to. And my wife doesn't mind me getting blood and scratches on this old fender!"

"Thanks for coming," I said. We talked for a moment about the deer herd, the mountain, possible snow. I was not interested in a long conversation in the cold.

Tacho and I shook his hand. "You're welcome back here next November, or before, if you shoot quail." I opened the old car door for him. "We'll have that cat by then; hopefully a lot sooner! Come by anytime."

Tacho and I watched his round taillights fade through his dust until they disappeared around the corner of the ridge.

"Damn!" I lamented. "We've been what, two winters now? Where did this come from?"

"Mexico!" Tacho gave me his deadpan look. "All the bad lions come from Mexico, that's what my *tía* says."

"I'm not going to mess with her," I smiled at him. I was never quite sure when Tacho was kidding, but he had made me feel a little better.

"You got a few minutes?" he asked me. "Let's go back in and talk this through."

"You bet!" I was eager to hear his thoughts.

Tacho followed me into the kitchen. Linnaeus was standing on the chair the hunter had vacated. Sara was helping him scoop applesauce and ground beef into his mouth; he waved a piece of bread at us and laughed. I waved back and he made a face.

I raised my eyebrows to Sara, realizing she had cooked the ground beef for Linnaeus while we gabbed in the dooryard with the hunter. "Thanks!" I mouthed.

Tacho and I continued on through the kitchen and down the hall to the living room. A big mesquite log filled the grate on the hearth and flames crackled up behind the screen. I pulled the screen aside and warmth flowed out. I slid a ladder-back oak chair onto the Navajo rug before the hearth and motioned for Tacho to do the same.

We warmed our hands and then talked for close to an hour. We heard Tacho's wife Sofia come into the kitchen, her daughter in tow; her greeting was followed by quiet conversation as she got the news about the lion from Sara.

When our plan was set, I threw another log on the fire, closed the screen, and Tacho and I walked slowly back down the hall to the kitchen.

The big bright kitchen held a different kind of warmth from the living room. The aroma of the stew simmering on the gas range flared our nostrils and fed our hearts even as our stomachs rumbled in anticipation.

Linnaeus had finished his supper and was asleep in his swing; Tacho's toddler sprawled snoring on Sara's wide lap. Sofia had pulled the cushioned bench from the window seat into the light and was stitching a three-corner tear, matching the thread as she went.

Sara held her index finger up to her lips to shush us.

Tacho and I watched Sofia finish her task; she returned the needle to her pocket sewing kit and motioned for Tacho to take Anita, his toddler, from Sara. Sara stayed in her chair while Sofia slipped Linnaeus from his swing without waking him and laid him on my shoulder. At my wife's urging she ladled a big crock of Sara's stew and covered it with wax paper.

Sofia and Tacho slipped out the door with their supper and their sleeping child; I put ours in his crib down the hall and came back for Sara. I ladled us a couple of bowls of stew, setting the stew pot in the fridge, ignoring Sara's frown at the gas it would take to cool it fast. I carried our bowls with spoons and napkins in by the fire.

I wanted to eat and get to bed. I was eager for dawn.

I don't remember sleeping that night, but I must have slept some because, when the alarm went off at four thirty, Sara was already up and gone. I pulled on my jeans and flannel shirt and found her in the kitchen, a coffee cake waiting for me, Linnaeus in his swing nibbling a hard-boiled egg.

"You're not supposed to be..." I began.

"Don't lay that big old lion hunter trip on me," she laughed, her eyes bright and her skin full of color. "Women have been having babies and cooking since Eve kissed that snake and lost her last true chance for romance."

"And men have been going off to the mountain to hunt. That's what I get for marrying a Barbarian from the Wild West. Remind me to call my mother."

She leaned over to kiss my cheek and poured me some coffee before she settled into her chair with a big mug of herb tea. We'd just started to eat when a cowboy knocked at the door.

I shouted "Okay!" and he clanged onto the kitchen with the stainless steel milk pail, uncovered and steaming in the cold blast that followed him. He set the pail on the maple drain board by the sink and tipped his hat to Sara.

"We got a lion. Killed a heifer," I greeted him. "Saddle up Mitch and Freckles; Tacho and I are going up country and see what's what."

"We may need you tomorrow." I added. "What you got planned?"

"Fence, pasture eight." The cowboy bit his tongue and his eyes grew wide. "Lion!" He took his hat off now and held it expectantly in both hands, smelling the coffee and the cake, waiting for an invitation to sit.

It did not come.

"Yeah, lion," I replied. "Stick close to Headquarters today and tonight and Tacho'll tell you what we need when we get back."

Sara nudged me with her foot under the table.

"Thanks." I realized I'd been a bit curt and I softened my voice. "Oh, and put my scabbard on my saddle. We'll be down in twenty. Tell your buddies to stick close too; maybe we'll all be going up there in the morning."

"Lion…" the cowboy murmured half to himself. "I seen a lion once, crost the road up in Wyoming; Jake said it was a bobcat but I seen that long tail goin' into the sage. Jake was drivin'. He hit the gas too late and it was gone 'fore I could get a shot off."

"You were carryin' your pistol then?" I queried him.

"Yeah, that was back before I got in that trouble." He grinned at us, his face red from the cold, his three top teeth missing. "Sorry, Ma'am," he nodded to Sara.

"Oh, Teeth", Sara flicked her hand at him. "That was way back in Texas. We know you're cured of that now."

"Yes, ma'am!" The cowboy, still hopeful for a slice of coffeecake, graced her with his full smile, bottom teeth black with tobacco stains.

"Sofia's got your bacon comin' in the bunkhouse," I couldn't help but smile, but I was not about to share our coffee and cake. "You hustle and get those horses ready for us. Put them in the Jeep; the rack's already on. We want to be up on top when the sun comes up."

"If those horses are ready when we get to the barn you can sleep tomorrow; Jake'll do the milking. You tell him so. Don't forget the scabbard. Now git!"

He recognized I wasn't really mad, so he laughed too, his mouth a bleak cavern. He replaced his hat on his slick hair on and was quickly out into the cold before another blast could hit us.

Sara shook her head. "Men!" she chuckled. "You know, you don't have to talk like your cowboys when you're around them; last I looked, gerunds still ended in 'g's." She pushed herself up out of her chair and waddled over to the drain board. "Or are you runnin' for some office in Texas?" she drawled.

She took a shallow white enamel pan from the shelf and set it in the sink. She poured the milk into it and busied herself at the counter.

I finished my half of the coffee cake and my coffee. I came up behind Sara and gave her a hug.

“I love you,” I whispered in her ear and took a tiny nip at the lobe.

“I love you too,” she whispered and turned around, leaning far forward so I could kiss her lips over her belly. “Be careful.”

“You know we will. Just another day on horseback.” I kept my voice low, hiding the adrenalin coursing through my veins. Or was it testosterone? Whatever, it had been a long night, my heart pounding in my head, my mouth dry in anticipation of the hunt.

I reassured Sara. “That lion has a lot more reasons to be scared of us than we have to be scared of her: Blue, Red, King, and Winchester, to start with.”

She tipped her head back and met my eyes, “You’re taking the dogs today? Don’t you and Tacho want to scope the terrain, and wait until tomorrow when you’ve got more men?”

I shook my head. “Snow’s coming anytime. We need to get up top with the horses while the trail’s still open. We want to come down on Cedar Spring, maybe take the lion by surprise where she’s holed up; get her running uphill, maybe treed.”

“Otherwise she’ll kill heifers all winter, and we’ll be bogged down in the canyon with the horses in the snow; that’s when it could get really dangerous.”

Tacho had shared this strategy with me the night before, but I let Sara’s eyes widen at my wisdom. I slid my arms from around her and smiled with all the confidence I could muster. “We’ll be home by three with a lion rug for you.”

Sara shook her head and said softly, "I don't want a rug. I want you. I want my babies to have a daddy when they grow up."

"Look, we got that old lion the first winter we had the place, no sweat." I pulled on wool socks and boots.

"It's only the old weak ones who take a beef, like I told the hunter. She'll probably roll over and die before we get there." I smiled to make my confidence stronger; this was my script and Sara knew it. It was an ancient ritual.

I tucked my vest under my arm and lifted my rough-out sheepskin coat from its hook by the door. I pushed my arms into its soft warm sleeves and grabbed my felt Stetson from the shelf above.

My wife handed me a couple of hard-boiled eggs, still warm, and a chunk of liverwurst wrapped in wax paper. I stuffed them in one pocket; Tacho would have both canteens ready at the barn.

I grabbed the doorknob to slip out into the predawn dark.

"Wait!" Sara called. She crossed the kitchen with a small black cloth packet in her hand. "Sofia left her sewing kit on the bench last night. Give it to Tacho for her."

"He won't see her 'til we get back!" I protested.

"Look, I just want to get it to her. I'll lose track of it here and I don't want Linnaeus to get into it. Put it in your pocket."

She did it for me, stuffing the little packet deep into my other coat pocket.

I grabbed my gloves and was out the door. I crossed the dooryard and stepped into my little adobe office back of the ranch shop. I flicked on the light, took the key from its hidden hook and unlocked my gun rack. I lifted my 30.30 carefully from its cradle; unlocked my file cabinet and took a full box of ammo from the drawer.

The cowboy was good as his word: our horses were already saddled and loaded in the back of the Jeep pickup, its horse rack still on board from fall roundup. I put my gun on the rack over the rear window and the ammo in the glove box.

Tacho was there with the dogs.

When my father owned the ranch, he relied on a professional lion hunter who brought his own pack of hounds. The first time Tacho and I had a lion, we called on this pro; but he took a week to get to us, and charged us a thousand dollars. By that time, the lion had killed twice again. The guy was arrogant as hell and his dogs were mangy and half-starved; Tacho and I decided we could hunt better ourselves and save money with dogs of our own.

So we bought a Redbone, a Bluetick and a Walker Hound from a breeder in New Mexico who kept an old toothless lion and trained hounds to track and tree. He cultivated their instinct to howl when they got a lion scent, so we could follow them on horseback.

Tacho kept the hounds in a run by the barn and let them out to race around Headquarters every few days. All three were good-natured young hounds; crazy for tracking, they ran off regularly but came back for supper, as there were no scents that interested them much this low on the range. They lived for lions.

They howled when we came anywhere near their run, but it was a soothing rather than irritating greeting, and they wagged their long tails furiously whenever they got the least attention.

Good big dogs.

Our hounds came with names--Red, Blue, and King. King, the Walker, was the biggest, tall and lanky and built to run. He outraced the other two when they romped in the corral and could give a horse a run for the money for the first hundred yards.

Their first winter the hounds paid for themselves: one lion killed a heifer in December; they tracked it and Tacho shot it clean as it cowered on a low limb of a Douglas Fir.

That lion had a mouthful of festered porcupine quills; it was nearly starved, unable to run a deer, so had turned to beef. A sad sight.

Another lion came though in March and the dogs tracked it but never found it; it killed just once and then disappeared. Tacho said it might have died of rabies or distemper; in any event, we gave the dogs credit for running it off.

None since.

Tacho had leashed the dogs with three of his long, braided lariats. They piled eagerly into the front seat of the Jeep, crowding between us, their breath steaming. They knew what was coming.

I drove out into the dark. The horses swayed in the bed as the Jeep growled up the steep mountain. Few hunters knew the back road to the ridge above Cedar Spring; we didn't see a soul or even a light all the way. The road was not on any maps and was a hard climb, even for a Jeep.

King poked his nose in my coat pocket, snuffing at the chunk of liverwurst in the wax paper. When I could take one hand from the wheel, I swatted him away lightly. He panted and grinned in the light from the dash.

I remembered the packet in my other pocket.

"Your wife left her sewing kit in the kitchen last night," I called to Tacho across the three squirming dogs. "I've got it in my pocket. Sara gave it to me to give to you. I don't know what she was thinking."

"Those kids keep them busy!" Tacho shouted back. "You've got another coming pretty soon; we've got one in the oven too! Sofia told me last night when we got home."

"Your wife worried about the cat?" he queried me.

"Some," I acknowledged. "I reassured her, but you know how they are."

"Sofia's uncle got raked by a cat once," Tacho raised his voice over the noise from the engine and the clattering horses. "Down in Mexico, they got a horse ranch; this lion came in May and took a foal. Her uncle went after it and cornered it and it came right at him. He just had a .22 and he put couple of slugs in its chest but it kept coming and got him good."

"Four long scars like knife wounds; I've seen them when he takes off his shirt."

"That cat would've killed him but the guy he was with swung his gun like an axe and caved in its skull."

"You get a clean shot today, you take it!" Tacho reminded me.

We drove on in silence. The dogs settled down and the only sounds were the rise and fall of the engine and the rattle of the horses as they kept their balance behind us. The Jeep's heater was not great, and frost crystals began to sparkle along the windshield's edge.

As we had hoped, we topped out just before dawn. The track ran along the crest of the Canciones and we had a clear view, a hundred or more miles east and west.

Down the western slope I glimpsed Headquarters. A curl of smoke rose from the chimney of the main house, nestled in the shadows; evidence Sara had stoked the fire in the living room, getting on with her day. I missed her all of a sudden and my heart caught in my chest as I thought of our warm kitchen.

I looked east. The round lid of the sun paused on a flat mesa way across the valley, as if waiting for its call to rise. It burned my eyes and I blinked hard. I focused on the track ahead.

We arrived at the flats above Cedar Spring and drove into the meadow at the west edge, silver with frost. Two deer startled up on the far side and disappeared into the pines.

No tracks cut the frost. The sun, responding to its call, rested a few degrees above the distant mesa. Its first rays sliced between the pines and stretched rainbow ribbons across the crystal meadow. No wind stirred the frozen grass.

We backed our horses down the drop gate and tightened their cinches. I loaded my lever action 30.30, but didn't chamber a cartridge as we had to ride some. I slipped the gun into its scabbard.

Tacho rode Freckles, a big Appaloosa mare, and I was on my Palomino, Mitch. We mounted quickly, alert to the slightest sound or movement in the pines.

Tacho kept the hounds on their tethers as we started down the switchbacks toward Cedar Spring.

We had ridden only a few hundred yards when the hounds went wild, baying and yanking at their tethers, racing back and forth in front of Tacho's horse. "They got the scent!" Tacho shouted back at me. "I'm going to let them off!"

He didn't have to dismount; he had doubled the lariat tethers and quickly released one end to let the hounds pull them through their collars. He instantly coiled his three lariats and tied them to the saddle straps by his right knee. Freckles crow-hopped sideways as the hounds raced past her into the pines.

The hounds were trained to flush the lion, get it running and give chase, baying, until it was treed or cornered. Then the timbre of their howling changed from a long bay to a high-pitched stream of short barks.

Our job was to listen; the lion might lead them back and forth across canyons or over ridges, but sooner or later the dogs would gain the advantage and bring her to bay.

Our biggest danger was that the lion would turn back and come at us and our horses. I rode Mitch up beside Tacho, pulled my gun from its scabbard and chambered a cartridge. We stood crosswise to the trail and scanned the mountainside up and down for any sign of movement, alert to each snapped twig.

Hunting deer with my father, I had occasionally experienced a heightened awareness during the chase, but never to the degree that lion hunting brought. Each nerve in my body felt charged; the morning light filtering through the pines took on a sharp clarity and my nostrils flared as if I could smell my prey.

Certainly if smell were the scent that mattered, our horses would smell the lion long before we did; their nostrils flared too and their ears pricked straight up, flicking from side to side like big antennae. They knew the hunt was on.

We did not have to wait for long. The baying traversed the mountainside to our south for a few minutes and then suddenly first one and then all the dogs changed the pitch of their cries. They were above us.

We wheeled our horses back up the switchbacks as quickly as possible. We rode into the meadow; the rainbows were gone, the yellow grass slick with moisture in the sun. A north wind had picked up. It stung my face and blew Tacho's hat off as we spun off the last switchback; it pressed us on as we galloped across the meadow.

We dove into the pines as the deer had earlier. The baying was still high above us. I rechecked the safety and slipped my gun back into the scabbard. I'd need both hands on the reins and saddle horn through the uneven pine stand. I reined Mitch back and kept a sharp eye out for deadfall. The last thing Mitch needed was a broken leg or a staub through his chest.

Tacho and I guided our horses up through the pines, ducking limbs and weaving past snags; the higher we climbed the thinner the stand grew. Old rockslides cut across our path and we picked our way gingerly across the scree.

Now we could see the terrain where the dogs were. Above the pines a knife-sharp ridge climbed toward a false summit; a cliff fell away to the west into the head of a box canyon. The only way up the ridge was along the east side, and it was almost too steep for the horses. Mitch stumbled to his knees and I pitched forward, my hat tumbled off, but I hung on as he scrambled back to his feet. I heard Freckles clatter up hard behind us; cascades of gravel whistled down the rock face.

I crested the false summit. The cat had gone as far as she could go. She was out on the limb of a big dead juniper, suspended over the cliff, silhouetted against the sky. Two hounds leapt at the base of the tree, baying furiously.

King lay crumpled on the scree.

"King!" I cried. I grabbed my saddle horn and started to swing off Mitch.

"No" Tacho shouted. "Stay on your horse! Shoot that cat!"

I wheeled in the saddle as he rode up next to me, his eyes wide, his hat gone.

"King!" I pointed to the brown and white form at the base of the tree.

"Shoot the goddamn cat!" Tacho shouted again. "Don't take your eyes off that cat! She'll come down the tree and kill those dogs and your horse and you before you can think 'I'm dead!' Shoot her! Now!"

I heard him. I wrestled my eyes off King and picked up the cat, snarling on the limb. It crept forward a foot, its long tail thrashing, shaking the dead tree like kindling.

I pulled my gun from the scabbard, thumbed the safety off, held my breath, drew a bead and squeezed the trigger. It took two seconds but it seemed an eternity.

The slug caught the cat in the chest, knocking her off the limb. She clung with her forepaws and the dogs leapt at her.

"Again!" Tacho screamed.

I worked the lever once quick; the spent cartridge spun past my ear.

The scene before me slowed. I counted each second as if it was an hour.

The big cat swirled beneath the limb. She showed her side and I drew a deep breath and held it; I found the bead and squeezed the trigger again; the kick of the recoil knocked me off balance in my saddle. Tacho's hand caught me as I fell back and kept me mounted; somehow I found my right stirrup and watched the scene unfold, each split second an eternity.

Red bloomed on the lion's side. Claw by claw she lost her grip on the limb. She stared pure hate at me, and then her eyes went out and the last claw sunk back and she tumbled into space, over and over slowly into the abyss. I had jacked the lever once more by instinct but didn't need another shot; I slipped my thumb under the hammer and eased it down, fingering the safety on.

Time snapped back. The two hounds raced along the cliff's edge, looking for a way down.

"Red! Blue! Back, now!" Tacho yelled and they gave up their frenzy and came to him, panting furiously. He was already off Freckles, his tethers in hand. He slipped loops through their collars, threaded the tied ends through and twitched them to his saddle horn. Freckles, feeling the pressure, stood stock still.

"King…" I moaned, looking down at last to the big brown and white dog by Mitch's front feet.

"Good work, good shot!" Tacho shouted. He too turned his attention to King. I dismounted and dropped the reins. Mitch stood rooted to the rock, his eyes rolling but his training solid.

The two shots echoed back and forth from ridge to ridge followed by eerie quiet. I shook my head to clear my vision and knelt by the broken dog.

"He's alive," Tacho said softly. He was kneeling too.

"She got him but he's still breathing." He stood up and pulled his canteen from his saddle.

I sat down cross-legged on the jagged stones and touched King's muzzle. He opened one eye and tried to lift his head. A thin whine escaped his lolling mouth. I caught a glimpse of his tail out of the corner of my eye as it raised once and fell back onto the stones.

"Good," Tacho whispered. "His back's not broke."

He knelt again close to King's ear. "Let me see your side, big fella," he crooned. "It's okay—that cat's gone to meet her maker—you're still with us." Tacho straightened up on his knees and crossed himself with his free hand. He unscrewed the cap to his canteen and took a big draught. His hand was shaking.

Tacho offered me the canteen and I took it, my hand shaking too. I gripped it tightly; I was perilously near the edge of the cliff and my instinct to protect our water kicked in. I looped the strap round my neck. My hat was back by the pines.

Tacho took a deep breath and let it out slowly. "OK, *bueno*," he said. "Now we think a minute."

I stroked King's head and Tacho ran his hand gently along the hound's ribcage. We watched the ribs shiver slowly up and then collapse down several times as the big hound struggled to breathe.

"Broken side down, but no blood on the rocks, that's good too," Tacho nodded slowly, feeling along King's spine. "We gotta turn him over, keep him warm, see if both lungs are working. Stay here a second."

Tacho quickly led both our horses away from the cliff and empty tree and rocks. He tied them to the first pine. He took the hounds' tethers from his saddle horn and led them a few yards further back along the edge of the shade, tying their tethers to two trees so they wouldn't tangle.

He ran to the edge of the pines and came back in a moment with my hat. He set it by the dogs and filled it with water from my canteen. The panting hounds eagerly lapped the water.

Tacho untied both our ponchos from our saddles.

I turned my attention back to King. He breathed hard and opened his eyes occasionally to look up at me. I stroked his head and sang the only song I could think of to him, a lullaby my mother once sang to me. His shivering was more pronounced.

Tacho was back. "Too cold here," he squatted down on his heels beside us. "We gotta get out of the wind, by the pines."

"Let's take a look, big boy," he whispered to King. He doubled over one poncho and laid it at King's back, and then gently scooped under the dog's shoulder and rump to roll him slowly over onto his other side.

King whimpered but his tail flopped weakly against the poncho as he lay on his good side.

"Ok, *bueno*," Tacho said again. My spirits lifted too for the first time since I saw King down. I could see his ribcage shuddering up on this side, too. Both lungs still worked.

My heart sank again as I focused more closely. The hound's sleek skin was peeled back like birch bark and a triangle of white felskin gleamed up at me, flecked with gravel like bubbles on surf. The patch was a foot long from top to bottom and half that along a jagged tear line just below King's spine.

"You almost dodged her, didn't you, big guy." Tacho sighed. Tears were streaming down the big man's cheeks; mine too, I suddenly realized.

"Good dog!" Tacho croaked. "We'll get you home; don't worry."

Tacho raised his eyes to meet mine. "What can we do?" he whispered to me, unconsciously trying to keep bad news from King. Tacho's brow knit, his hat line a pale stripe below his jet black hair. "He's in shock; he's got his blood but that skin'll be dead in a minute; we'll never get him home."

"The needle! The thread!" I blurted.

"Qué?" Tacho gave me a quizzical look, his head tipped a fraction to one side.

"The tear in the cushion." I practically shouted. "I've got her kit!"

"We can sew him up!" I was so excited I almost leapt to my feet. I dug deep in my right pocket, pulled out liverwurst and an egg. They tumbled to the scree.

Tacho looked at me as if I had gone insane. He held the dog on the poncho, as King was suddenly struggling to get up, sensing my excitement.

I reached way down into my left pocket and felt the packet Sara had stuffed into it less than two hours earlier. I pulled it out and held it high like the chalice of Christ. "We've got what we need! King, you're going to make it home!"

"Oh God, oh Sara, what were you thinking?" I babbled like a man possessed.

Tacho suddenly nodded too. "*Caballero!*" he exclaimed.

"Yes, yes!" I shouted to the sky, my mind racing back to the semester of basic veterinary at Cornell. "We can do this!"

"Ok, boss, I'm your nurse now," Tacho laughed with me, eyes dancing, tears of joy now flowing. "I'll get the smear; give me that pack before you fling it over the cliff and I have to make you climb down after it!"

I gladly relinquished the packet and Tacho slipped it in his hip pocket. He leapt up and raced back to his saddlebag. While he was gone I said a quick prayer of gratitude for Sara and Sofia. I threw in a word for Tacho, too, and then I prayed for strength and faith for King and me. "Hang in there, pal," I whispered to him.

Tacho returned in a moment with a half-pint tin of iodine and the swab we used to wipe barbed wire cuts on cattle. He and I always carried a swab kit but we'd never until now carried needle and thread.

We lifted King gently, cradled in the poncho, and moved him carefully from the cliff's edge. He weighed at least a hundred pounds so we watched our footing; we laid the makeshift stretcher on a patch of moss in the shade at the edge of the pines.

The horses and dogs watched our every move, nickering and whining their curiosity.

Tacho carefully doused the wound with canteen water and we picked out the gravel; what we missed would work its way through over the years. Tacho sterilized Sofia's needle and thread and smeared a thick line of iodine along the edge of the skin. I folded the skin back over the wound, careful to line up the black and brown markings on King's side.

The skin had already started to stiffen so we kneaded it gently, constantly, with water and iodine smear as I sewed along the edges.

The needle had no curl, but fortunately the hound's skin was ample, and I could wrinkle it enough to draw the needle in and out. It took me close to an hour; the work was painstaking and King's shivering created a moving target. Tacho rubbed the big hound's legs and wrapped the poncho around his head. He reassured King softly in English and Spanish and the singsong voice he used to cajole horses as he shod them.

At last we were done. I breathed deeply and stood up and stretched my aching icy fingers. Tacho swabbed the whole scar again with iodine and replaced the packet and the tin in his saddlebag.

We were out of water. Tacho wrung out my hat and blocked it back into shape; he set it on my head and grinned at me. "Half way there, boss!"

King indeed had one more agony to endure. Tacho made a sling from his lariats and his poncho, securing the corners with bowline loops and covering the big hound with my poncho.

It was makeshift at best. We used my rope to suspend the cradle from both saddles and led the horses in tandem back through the pines, Tacho walking carefully by the poncho sling to keep it from swinging against the trees or dumping the dog to the ground. It was all downhill, but steep; we picked our way and it took time. It was late morning when I finally saw the pines thin and the light from the meadow.

We cradled King in the ponchos on the Jeep seat. His breathing was steady and he had stopped shivering, content to rest. The other hounds leapt into the back of the Jeep and we closed the gate.

I unloaded my 30.30 and rested it on the rack. Now that the risk of meeting the lion was past, Tacho could ride Freckles home, and he did, leading Mitch. He retrieved his hat and set off down the switchbacks toward Cedar Spring.

Tacho got home before I did. I drove slowly, as every bump jarred King. When I finally came up the driveway everyone was waiting, Tacho in a clean shirt and fresh Levi's, Sofia and Sara and the babies, and all three cowboys. Sara greeted me with a long hug; her face was streaked but her tears were past.

She turned her attention to King. "I called the vet and she's on her way," she reported. "I hear you pulled the rabbit out of the hat once again!"

We all lifted King from the front seat of the Jeep and carried him into the living room by the fire. Tacho and Sofia took the ponchos and lariats, and we invited the cowboys in to check out the stitched wound before they returned to work.

They all admired the stitching; Jake asked if he could come by the office someday and learn how to do it. Sofia told him she'd give him lessons and we all laughed, relieved that King was home at last, safe, warm.

I sent the three cowboys on an afternoon expedition up the box canyon to retrieve the lion carcass. The cat was big and healthy and her pelt would become the rug for King to lay on, by my desk in my office.

Tacho, Sofia, Sara and I took the rest of the day off. We carried big bowls of leftover stew into the living room and kept watch over King until the vet arrived. Red and Blue perched outside on the porch, their big paws on the windowsills that framed the hearth, whining and watching our every move. Hounds never came inside—a tradition King broke that day—and his brethren would not be so lucky.

The vet arrived and got King up; she gave him a little water and an antibiotic shot and checked my work. "No need to redo that," she said. "It's not cosmetic but it'll hold. Why didn't you change thread color when you got to that big brown patch?"

I grinned like an idiot and Tacho rolled his eyes.

"Seriously, though," she added, "You no doubt saved his life. He'll not hunt again, that tear will always be stiff and I don't want him running for a long time. Keep him indoors and keep him warm. He's earned it."

She stroked King's ears and nuzzled him with her nose. "Haven't you, you good big dog?"

King lifted his muzzle and a soft sweet howl escaped his throat. His big tail slapped the Navajo rug.

Ten years have passed since that day.

Tonight, I listened to the November wind howl and watched Andrea and King roll on the soft old rug. She scratched his belly, careful to avoid the wrinkled scar. He howled his softest note and licked her face. He had proclaimed himself her protector from the moment Sara and I brought her home from the hospital, three days before the winter solstice. He licked her face then, too, and growled deep in his chest if we chastened him, grinning and wagging his tail all the while, as if to say, "Only kidding."

Tonight, flames flowed up and warmth streamed out from a big mesquite log on the hearth, just as they had that night when Tacho and I planned our hunt as Sofia stitched the cushion in the kitchen and talked babies with Sara.

All of us made that hunt a success. Blue and Red were long gone, but King's presence still filled our room and our hearts.

"Bedtime, you two!" I advised Andrea and her first love. They rolled their eyes at me, stood up and stretched, and wandered down the hall to their room, the old dog a little unsteady, the young girl prancing by his side.

COUNTY FAIR

Each December, enterprising feed and farm equipment stores in San Kino County mailed their ranch customers new calendars with the third Thursday in April circled.

Opening day for the County Fair!

Judging from the crowds that streamed through the wide chain-link gates just south of the tracks, plenty of households in town circled this Thursday, too.

On this day, our ancient cattle truck made its annual pilgrimage to town. We arrived early. Linnaeus and Tacho's daughter Anita clambered in and out of the truck while we waited for the chute, making sure their 4-H steers had water and grain and stayed as clean as possible. When they weren't fussing with their steers, they swirled around the corrals, checking out the competition.

After what seemed an interminable wait, just before noon it was our turn to unload. Craning my neck, I watched the loading chute shake in my cracked mirrors, growing larger as I slowly backed the truck between pickups and stock trailers. Linnaeus and Anita stood on either side of the truck, urging me back, gesturing like an airport flight line crew guiding a jumbo jet to its gate.

I set the truck against the chute, locked the brakes and gears and killed the engine. Anita and Linnaeus scrambled into the back of the truck, untied their steers and led them down the chute and into the cavernous 4-H Hall.

As soon as they were clear I started up again and pulled away, relinquishing the chute for the next truck and its cargo of 4-H teens with their steers or pigs or horses.

The fairgrounds had been an airport during the war and the 4-H hall was an old quonset hut hanger. By day, the interior had an undersea aspect, as lime-colored light filtered down from fiberglass panels high overhead. Pinprick holes in the old roof pushed pencils of yellow light through the dust. Dim dimes at their tips slid across the oiled floors and stalls all afternoon as the pencils angled east.

The interior was never truly bright. After dark, strings of flyspecked bulbs took over.

Fifty weeks of the year this cavernous hanger lay empty, but on the third Thursday of April, hours before the general admission gates opened at five, it became a landlocked Noah's ark, filled with sounds and smells of the steers, pigs, sheep, ducks, rabbits and other creatures the 4-H'ers gathered into its hold.

While I parked the truck, Anita and Linneaus led their steers through the crisscross aisles to the section reserved for their Cancione 4-H Club. They tethered the two, forked mountains of fresh straw all around them, and then ran back through the maze and out into the dust and sun. By the time they found the truck, I had unloaded four burlap feedbags and their heavy rubber feed and water buckets.

They helped me slide a battered steamer trunk from the truck's bed. It was filled with everything their 4-H club members would need for the week ahead.

Together we trundled the lot into the hall on the dolly the Fair provided. Linnaeus and Anita were excited. They had both turned thirteen the previous fall. These were their first steers to the Fair.

My mind rewound to shipping day the previous November, when the two straddled the chute for hours as hundreds of steers streamed beneath them, seeking two perfect calves to fatten for April. They seemed suspended in time. A generation before, I, too, dangled from the same fences, picking my 4-H steers. Tacho the horseman, born on a ranch west of town, rode high school rodeo at the Fair through the same era.

Last November, Anita chose her steer early and then shouted advice to Linnaeus throughout the afternoon as he wrestled to decide. He finally pointed a steer out to Tacho and me as we worked the scales, shouting "That one! The one with the fat rump! Don't let him go!"

I shouted back, "You grab him, they don't bite!" and Linnaeus vaulted into the chute and wrapped his arms around his steer's neck to hold him back from the scales until we dropped the gate.

We weighed the steer alone: two hundred and twenty pounds. Linnaeus bought him with cash at the day's steer rate; it was his first entry in a folding file that now bulged with receipts and records.

By the third Thursday in April, Anita's and Linnaeus' steers weighed over a thousand pounds.

All afternoon members of the Cancione 4-H Club swarmed around their section of the hanger. More steers lumbered into stanchions beneath the Club's green and white banner. The whole hanger buzzed with excitement; more than 20 livestock-based 4-H clubs, each a dozen or so members, had reserved space. Almost everyone had arrived by the time the main gates opened.

Families trickled in to join their sons and daughters; they leaned on the pine slats that delineated each club's turf and gossiped about the minutiae of ranch life. I caught up with my neighbors. Shortly after five, Tacho arrived with Sara and Sofia.

We strolled along the line of stanchions, commenting on the multitude of Hereford, Angus, Charolais, Shorthorn and Barzona steers, their coats sleek for Saturday's show, their owners hovering.

One stanchion in Cancione's section was still vacant.

"Hey Linnaeus," I shouted over the backs of the steers. "Who's missing?"

"Jasmine," he shouted back. "Anita tried to call her from the payphone; no answer."

Tacho glanced at me and raised one eyebrow. We all knew Jasmine, and we knew her mother, too. I shrugged and Tacho smiled and shook his head. We continued our stroll. Sofia and Sara were down the row chatting with a couple of tourists, a man in baggy shorts and woman in tight jeans. They had missed our exchange.

Our small group moved past the beeves and the sheep and came into the section reserved for the pigs. A couple of younger Cancione members had porkers, and another club always brought their big Hampshire sow with her piglets. Sara and Sofia were kneeling by the slats, reaching through to scratch the big sow's broad head. Her huge ears drooped and she rolled her eyes with pleasure.

Tacho and I came up behind our wives. "That's your next purse!" I teased Sara.

"You!" She flung over her shoulder, laughing at me. "You probably want to make this big lady into footballs!"

"Aren't those babies the cutest things?" she went on. "Twelve of them: and I think I've got problems!"

"You're built a little different," I allowed. She ignored me.

Sofia stood up and stretched and linked her arm through Tacho's. "Remember when my auntie fixed those pigs' ears for us? And cracklings? They were so good! You ate about a dozen!" Tacho smiled and nodded but held his peace. He was happy to let Sofia carry the conversation for both of them.

Just past the sow, along the end of the hanger, another club had set up a small petting zoo. So far, two pot-bellied pigs were its only occupants. The tourists Sara had been talking with stepped into the pen and approached the little pigs as cautiously as if they were javelina. "Watch where you step," the man called out. "There's poo everywhere,"

"No, Pooh's the bear," Sara whispered in my ear. "These are Piglets." She took pity on the tourists and stepped into the pen with them. "Don't worry," she reassured them. "These little guys are friendly as lap dogs."

"Smarter, too," she added.

The end of the hanger suddenly boomed. What was that?" the tourists exclaimed in unison and startled back from the pigs. "Thunder?"

"Not in April!" I responded. "The sun's shining; that's someone banging on that tin door."

My answer was confirmed when we heard a shout from outside the hanger, "Open the goddamn door! I don't have all day!"

Before we could react the baggy-shorted tourist leapt across the pen, loosed the bolt and rolled the tall door aside.

"No! I shouted. "Leave that shut! Are you nuts, the pigs'll get out!"

The door faced west. As it rolled open, the sun blinded us all for a second. The two pot-bellied pigs darted into a shady corner the sun's onslaught missed.

I knew the voice from outside. It seemed as though I'd tried without success all my life to escape that particular voice. At least I wasn't alone; I remembered with some relief that Tacho, Sofia and Sara would recognize the voice too, even though they had only known her for a decade or two:

Tillie.

Tacho and I sprang over the fence to keep the pigs cornered while Sara raced across the pen to close the door.

She was too late. "You touch that door, girlie, I'll whack your knuckles with this two by four; I've been waitin' by that friggin' chute for an hour! I know this old hut better'n they do; we're comin' in right here!" Tillie rasped.

There was no mistaking Tillie. She wedged a rough-cut timber in the gap to keep the big door ajar and shouted over her shoulder, "Open the gate, honey, bring him in!"

I shaded my eyes and squinted into the glare. A battered stock trailer angled from an old Buick wagon about ten feet outside the hanger. Tillie had backed right into the adjacent corral and was set to unload, but the trailer's gate swung out, so she needed to stop short of the door.

The sun lit up Tacho and me, targets for Tillie. She recognized us instantly. “Hey, you cowboys,” she yelled, “give Jasmine a hand there, she’s got her blue ribbon steer all set and we’re comin’ in!”

“Dammit, Tillie, there’s pigs in here, you can’t just back in anywhere you want!” I shouted.

“Always have!” She cackled. “I recall backing into you a few times, partner!”

Tillie, fully in control now, rolled the door wide open and the beam clattered to the cement floor.

“Oops. Sorry, missy,” she shouted to Sara. She recognized her in the light, remembering who she was, “That was before your time,” she added, grinning at my wife. Tacho burst out laughing next to me, and Sofia cupped her hands over her mouth, her ample frame shaking with mirth at Tillie’s performance. Even Sara was smiling; she knew Tillie all too well.

The two tourists didn’t see anything to laugh at, and neither did I. They stood dumbfounded, their eyes wide, watching me try to keep the pigs cornered. I slipped in the manure they had pointed out a few seconds earlier and caught myself on the fence before stumbling back into the sun.

“Lookit him,” Tillie addressed her audience like the director of a star-studded performance, “Red as a beet! You gotta stay outta the sun, mister.”

Beyond Tillie, Jasmine and her two younger sisters stood poised by the trailer gate. At Tillie’s shout the little girls swung it open and Jasmine’s big Black Angus steer lumbered out. Jasmine stood ready with the halter.

"Omigod, it's a bull!" the man in the shorts shrieked. He picked up the two-by-four Tillie had used to jam the door and swung it at the steer's nose, missing by several feet. Jasmine ducked aside. The tourist danced around between the steer and Tillie, trying to set himself for another swing. The steer cocked its head to one side and peered questioningly at Jasmine, spooked by this crazy human bouncing in the bright sunlight.

"Run!" the man shouted. "I'll hold him off!"

Tillie was laughing but she could see potential for danger here. She barked at the man, "Gimme that goddamn club, mister, I been to the rodeo, I'll save your ass!" She grabbed the timber from him as if stripping an orchestra conductor of his baton. "You jump up on that fence over there 'til we get this beast under control."

The tourist scrambled past the Buick, leaving his companion standing alone in the center of the petting zoo.

"Put the halter on him, Jasmine, honey," Tillie went on. She leaned against the side of the big steer to keep him squared-up to the trailer.

The pigs saw their chance and bolted past me through the open door. They caught sight of the big steer and skidded to a standstill just as he saw them. He swung his head away from the halter before Jasmine could loop it around his nose.

"Wait, Nero!" Jasmine wheedled, but it was too late. The steer lowered his head and lumbered toward the two little pigs. They wheeled and raced back into the hanger, past the woman in the tight jeans standing frozen in place, and pressed themselves against the gate to the aisle at the far side of the little corral.

The steer gained momentum as he came through the door and crossed the petting zoo. He also sidestepped the tourist, his eyes focused on the pigs. He lowered his head until his nose was practically scraping the cement floor. With a 'whump!' that echoed like a bass drum through the cavernous hall he pinned the pigs against the gate, and immediately lost traction in the slimy manure.

The big steer went down on his knees.

The pigs screamed bloody murder. Jasmine and her sisters raced into the hanger. Tillie slid the door shut and bolted it behind them.

"Piece o' cake! she beamed. "Nero, leave those poor little piggies alone."

"You, you big injun, stop your laughin' and tend to the lady," she threw this in Tacho's direction, "while we women get some control back into this goddamn faerie circle."

Drawn by the commotion, a small crowd began to gather in the aisle beyond the gate. Sofia and Sara rescued the pigs as Tillie and Jasmine slipped the rope halter over the steer's nose and up behind his ears. The teens who owned the little pigs worked their way to the front of the crowd, confirmed their pigs were safe for the moment and, at a word from Sara, raced back through the little crowd to retrieve wet towels.

Haltered, the big Black Angus steer staggered back to his feet and shook his head, sending spit flying. He wheezed to clear his nose, rubbing his face against Jasmine's hip. She scratched his neck between his ears beneath the rope halter.

"Lookit him," Tillie turned her accusing gaze back on me. "Now we gotta wash him all over again; his knees are all shit up; can't you even keep a coupla pigs under control?"

"Men!"

Everyone in the aisle cracked up at this and I stood with my hands on my hips.

"Tillie, can't you just come in the main door like everybody else?" I sputtered. "And you're four hours late."

"Oh, no!" Tillie pouted at me. "Late again! And you told me you was gonna wear two rubbers last time!"

Sara shot me a look that said, "Don't dig yourself in any deeper." She cuddled one little pig, who appeared to have suffered no harm; thanks to the slippery floor, the big steer's hooves had found no traction. Sofia cradled the other squirming pig in one arm like a big puppy and mopped her brow with her sleeve.

The woman in the tight jeans still stood alone in the center of the pen. She relaxed a bit and looked around. "Max?" she called tentatively.

"Oh honey, we left him outside," Tillie smiled broadly at her. "You don't need him, come on with us down to the midway with some real women, we'll have a coupla beers and some fried dough. Let him find us. If'n he loves ya, he'll be back; if he don't, he ain't worth your time."

Tillie strode to the center of the pen and clapped the woman on the shoulder, her hand still soaked from sliding the halter over Nero's nose. Her handprint lay like a red passion flower on the woman's pink blouse.

Tillie scooped the tourist toward the gate. By this time Jasmine and her sisters, with Anita, Linnaeus and the rest of their club, had led Nero to his stanchion. The pigs' owners reappeared with wet towels for their piglets, and Sofia and Sara.

Sofia and Sara held the two potbellied pigs while we drew the gate closed, and then slipped through to join us after settling the pigs back on the floor of their pen and wiping their hands and arms clean. Tacho and I joined them to follow the rest of the crowd. We all gathered under the green and white Cancione banner.

After a couple of nervous glances over her shoulder, the tourist seemed one of us.

Tillie, as always, held center stage.

Sheriff Gant strode down the aisle. "Tillie, your Buick is right in the lane out there…" he started, but Tillie smiled her sweetest and stepped forward to greet him, leaning in as if to give him a hug and kiss. He shied back.

"Keys are in the ignition, sweetie," she reached out and pinched his badge to hold him from backing away. "Protect and serve, baby. I protected this poor lady here from these dirty ol' cowboys, so now it's your turn to serve. Pull that four-holer into the lot for me, okay?" She raised her eyebrows and leaned forward a bit. "Worth your while!" she cooed.

Tillie released his badge and Gant was glad to go.

I just shook my head in awe.

Tillie had a big ranch just south of us in the Canciones, right along the border. We grew up together; she inherited her ranch about the time I bought mine from my father.

Our parents had been close, but Tillie and I were not. Like all of us, she always wore Levi's over boots, but from the time she turned twelve in sixth grade her jeans got tighter every year. Since that year, her trademark was always a brief halter top and a silver and turquoise cornflower necklace. She loved to lean across my desk in eighth grade, driving me nuts; she had no tan line and we all knew why.

Tillie rolled and smoked her own brand of tobacco, a habit that over the years had deepened her distinctive raspy voice, but she could still run a mile and drink any cowboy under the table. She spent four years at the University while I was back East.

Now she raised top quality Angus. She was still, as Sara put it, drop dead gorgeous.

Men, especially married men, had a way of disappearing from the County if they got too close to Tillie. Her three daughters looked different enough so we were pretty sure they had three different fathers; every man I knew was glad none of them looked like him.

All her girls were smart and extroverted; I could see the same dynamic setting up between Linnaeus and Jasmine that I remembered from my high school years with Tillie in the Cancione 4-H Club.

Two of five years, my Herefords beat her Angus, and Tillie had her own brand of revenge. I made myself a mental note to have a talk with Linnaeus. All the young people stayed with their calves at night; one parent stayed, too, to chaperone. Sara had shown me the list, but I had no idea who got the first night. Not me, and, I hoped, not Tillie.

All the calves were settled. Outside, it was getting dark. A blonde Pie-eyed Piper, Tillie led us all out of the hanger. In the arena behind the grandstand, we could hear the booming exhausts and metal shrieks from the Demolition Derby, but it was the midway that caught the 4-H'ers' eyes.

In the distance, we spotted the Ferris wheel sparkling above the dust; the air smelled of cotton candy; stuffed pandas bobbed atop the concessions. Sara took my hand and squeezed it. “Good catch!” she whispered in my ear.

“You too!” I smiled at her in the gathering dusk. Another year, another County Fair begun.

BOX CANYON

At the end of fall roundup, Tacho and I released sixty weaned heifers into Lookout Pasture. The high country was ideal for the sturdy young cattle and—as long as the mountain lions had plenty of deer for dinner—safe.

Our practice was to put our replacement heifer calves as far from the bulls as possible and let them grow up for a year and a half. A pregnant yearling risked an early grave for both herself and her calf, a loss Tacho and I had witnessed too often in our early years on the ranch. It pained our hearts and broke our wallets; even if we were lucky and the heifer and her calf survived, pulling the calf left us raw and bruised and exhausted. After a dozen years, we were tired of these adventures; and smarter, too. We kept our heifers far from harm.

Eighteen months passed from the end of fall roundup.

I remember lots of little details from that particular April morning. We had gathered fifty-six of the two-year-old heifers the week before. These were now settled in Headquarters Pasture, getting used to horses and fences. The last four were still hiding on the mountain.

An hour before dawn that Monday, Tacho and I led our horses through the barnyard. We left the horse trailer parked and cajoled our horses to step up and squeeze into the stock trailer, which we had hitched to the Jeep pickup. We loaded ten sections of steel fence and a bale of hay into the frame set on the pickup bed, and set out for Box Canyon. We figured our four stray heifers might have spent the night near the trough by the windmill where the canyon widened into its delta: if so, they'd hear us coming and retreat upstream to hide.

This particular morning we had a rare advantage, as a few drops of rain had fallen overnight, and the heifers' tracks on the canyon floor would be clear as typeface on bond paper. The night was cool, but we had our windows down. The desert smelled sage-sweet after the rain, and Tacho and I felt good. We carried hot coffee in our thermoses, and in the wooden toolbox on the seat between us, my pot roast sandwich and his burrito wrapped in wax paper.

Two miles of Jeep road wound up from the bajada to the windmill, and as we clattered eastward the sky over the mountain brightened from gunmetal gray to rose in our windshield. The sun cracked over the ridge just as we led our horses from the trailer and tethered them to the mesquite tree by the trough.

Four sets of cloven hoof prints rewarded us. We pivoted the long stock trailer around and eased it forty feet or so up the narrowing canyon. We linked the fence sections together to make a lane into the trailer. As we expected, the heifers had retreated up the draw. Their tracks were big and deep and well-spaced in the damp sand.

We figured we could corner the heifers near the top of the canyon and turn them back toward the well. Their curiosity would get the better of them. They'd snuff at the steel fence and nudge the open gate to the stock trailer, barriers they hadn't encountered since they were calves. To lure them into the trailer, I gathered a couple of flakes of alfalfa hay we'd jammed in between the fence sections and threw them forward into the nose of the trailer. The way we planned it, in a couple of hours our heifers would be pushing each other aside to get at that hay instead of turning back on us and our horses.

Year after year, the last heifers always fell for the "hay in the trailer" trick. We felt confident we'd have them in Headquarters Pasture by noon. We'd leave the fence sections for the moment, as Lookout Pasture would be empty until fall. We would bring our horses home in the back of the Jeep.

Everything should have worked out just like that.

We chuckled as our horses laid their ears back and glared at the fresh hay. They pulled at their tethers.

"No such luck," I whispered to them. "You'll get yours later if you do your job right."

Tacho and I sat on the Jeep tailgate and drank some coffee. The pale gold sunrise flooded the canyon and lapped over the barrel cacti that lined its rocky banks, transforming their spines into crowns of curled crystals. Tacho ate half his burrito, put the rest in his saddlebag, and braided a little more of his new lariat. Way above us, a Canyon Wren's cascading song greeted the day, and in the trough a bullfrog croaked. A little breeze stirred past us from the valley, headed for the cliff a mile or so to the east at the head of Box Canyon.

The heifers were in no hurry and neither were we. We didn't want to spook them; we'd rather let them get used to our smell on the breeze. I finished my coffee and put the thermos back in the Jeep. I untied the big bay horse

I was riding. He was stubborn and hostile, but fearless. Although he probably had a name, Tacho always called him "Blockhead" and that's how I remember him. I looped my canteen strap over the pummel, kneed Blockhead softly in the belly so he blew, tightened the cinch and swung into the saddle.

Tacho rode Rose, a smart skittish Appaloosa mare. We headed up the draw, following the heifers' tracks. It was easy.

Tacho was a good tracker. He told me once he saw the tracks in his mind. I understood what he meant: tracking is one-quarter skill and three-quarters art. A good tracker has sharp eyes with a soft focus that takes in the whole picture that unfolds across the landscape.

I learned lots from Tacho. I watched him follow the tracks, recording in my memory what I observed for those instances when I had to track alone.

We had ridden about two hundred yards and had just crossed a tabletop of flat smooth granite where no tracks were visible. My eyes were already on the sandy streambed beyond the rocks where the heifers' tracks reappeared, cutting black shadows in the white sunlit sand, when Rose stopped short and Tacho put out his hand to keep us from passing. I look at him and then followed his eyes and gesture as he pointed to the shade along the edge of the streambed.

I half expected to see a sleepy rattlesnake, which would not have been a big surprise after the April shower, but worthy of our caution.

I saw no snake, but what I did see sent a cold shiver down my spine and made the short hairs on my neck stand on end: one small, clearly-outlined barefoot print, evidence that a person had crossed the sand since the night rain.

We seldom encountered people on the ranch, and when we did, it was not good news. Besides ranchers, four types of people came and went in the desert: rustlers, miners, birdwatchers and immigrants.

Rustlers operated at night. Miners, or rock hounds as we called them, were generally hermits who avoided us, and we, them. Some prospectors were crazy enough to take a wild shot at someone who stumbled onto their claim, but we knew where they lived in their tents or shacks, and we worked around them. Birdwatchers didn't watch where they put their feet or hands, or where they sat, and so got snakebit from time to time.

Immigrants presented the most complex challenge. Most came north from the cities of Central and South America and knew little of the desert; they suffered from hunger and thirst and exposure, and their so-called guides, or "*coyotes,*" were generally unsavory bandits driven by greed. A recipe for tragedy.

In the flat grassland along the San Kino River, we saw their tracks and occasionally crossed paths with them, but not in the mountains, and never barefoot.

This small person—likely a child—was by all evidence alone: neither rustler not rock hound nor birdwatcher.

Tacho dismounted quietly and dropped Rose's reins to the flat rock. She stood stock still as trained. He carefully stepped along the fringe of the granite to where the shade began and squatted at the boundary. He took off his straw hat, pulled a clean white handkerchief from his hip pocket and wiped his brow. He let his eyes adjust to the shade, and then scanned the banks of the wash up and down first the north side, and then the south.

I searched for a sign of the child from my vantage point atop Blockhead. I saw nothing. The air was still and silent, and heat waves shimmered off the rocks where the morning sun, higher in the sky every minute, beat down. I saw flickers of dragonflies moving in and out of the shade, and a Tanager flashed across the stream way ahead, but I saw nothing that appeared unusual. Somewhere, though, was a barefoot person. Downwind: watching us?

Five minutes passed. Tacho finally stood and walked over to me. "Okay, *bueno*," he said quietly. "This fellow came from the water and stayed on the edge. He stepped on the stones all the way except right there."

"He crossed up there," the tall Mexican motioned with his hat to a jumble of boulders about forty feet upstream, "and went into that brush."

"Unless he's got feet of steel he's right there now. He's maybe not wearing any clothes; there's no threads on those prickers," he motioned to a line of manzanita overhanging the granite, "but you can see he brushed them 'cause they're bent. I bet there's blood but I'm not going to look."

"You stay here."

This was one of Tacho's longer speeches in the years we'd worked together and I knew he was serious. I nodded. He put his hat back on, took his canteen off his pommel and walked upstream to the boulders. He stopped in the sun. "*Chico*!" he shouted into the brush. "*Vente 'ca! No soy migra*!"

Silence. "*Te veo*!" Tacho shouted into the brush. "*Tengo agua bueno. Sé que tienes hambre. Tengo un burrito para tí!"*

Moments passed in silence. Tacho stood like a statue in the streambed. Rose swished flies off Blockhead's face with her tail. He sighed and blew. I waited and watched the brush.

After what seemed an eternity I saw a movement and a small boy emerged and stood cautiously at the brink where the shade met the sun. He wore only a ragged pair of briefs, a flash of white against his dark skin.

"*Bueno*," Tacho said quietly. I barely heard him. He walked slowly over to the boy, who stood still. I could hear murmurs as they talked for a moment. The boy sat down on one of the boulders in the shade. Tacho gave him a drink from his canteen. More murmurs.

The boy stayed where he was and Tacho walked back to me. "He's okay," he said. "His sister's in there, too. We'll take them back to the ranch."

I met his eyes. "Mexicans?" I asked.

Tacho gave me a look as if I had been born on the moon. Obviously my question didn't merit an answer but he provided one anyway. "Guatemalan," he said softly, so the boy couldn't hear. "You ever see a Mexican looked like that?" He motioned slightly with his head toward the boy, "You're riding the right horse this morning, *vaquero*!"

“He walks out to the road and hitches a ride to the Mission to borrow a pistol from his priest.” (Gun Shop)

“Today when I woke up it felt like home.” (Windmill Tower)

“It was as though Goya shook out his paintbrush on the desert, except a hundred times brighter under the cobalt sky.” (Good Neighbor)

"If there's anywhere in the world kids should feel safe,
it's at school." (Powder Keg)

Above the pines a knife-sharp ridge climbed toward a false summit; a cliff fell away to the west into the head of a box canyon." (Lion Hound)

"You don't need him, come on with us down to the midway with some re
women, we'll have a coupla beers and some fried dough." (County Fair)

"I say a prayer of gratitude for rain and sunshine, family and home and all that remains good in the world." (Box Canyon)

“Early August, the heart of rainy season.” (“Coyote Music”)

"In the winter, Tacho's uncle Elijah lived in the County Jail. He built fence for us from March until the first snow." (Fence Line)

"That's JR's truck," I said.
"And he's up to no good, you can bet." (Bad Cowboy)

“Tacho took care of the horses.” (Shoe Loose)

“Drought plagued the ranch.” (False Witness)

“Eventually rain returned to the ranch,
but Nora never did.” (False Witness)

“This was one of my favorite spots, and whenever I had an excuse to come here I liked being alone for a few minutes.” (Sound Water)

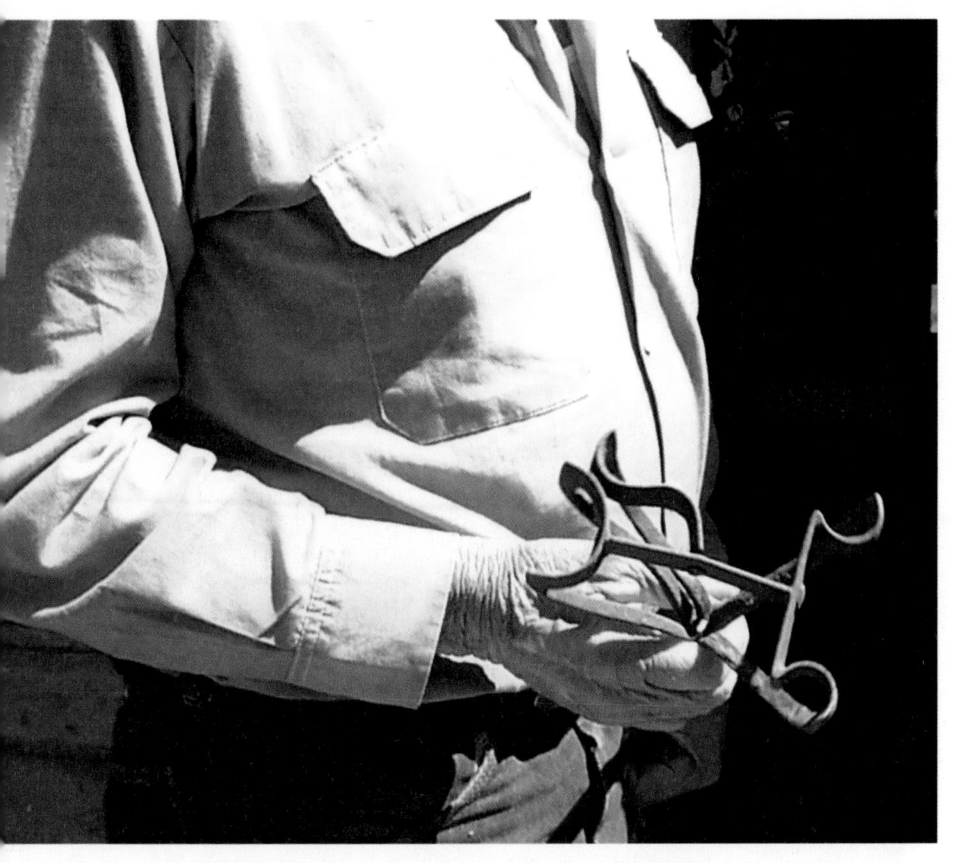

“It was time to brand.” (Branding Fire)

“Truth.” (Branding Fire)

Vaquero was the moniker Tacho usually reserved for eastern dudes. I caught his irony and smiled. He forgave me with a slight twitch of one eyebrow and became serious again, speaking louder so the boy would hear, "*Déme su poncho, caballero, por favor.*"

Tacho made this request of me formally in Spanish to acknowledge our relationship aloud to the boy, who was watching us warily, listening closely.

I recognized the symbolism of the poncho. To share it would be the first step toward restoring dignity for the children. I nodded and untied my poncho from the back of my saddle's cantle. Tacho walked upstream and presented the garment to the boy, formally, like a royal robe. The child disappeared into the thicket.

Tacho returned to the horses and untied his poncho. He spoke softly, "The horses will be okay by the water. The *coyote's* gone. He was up the cliff anyway."

"We'll take the two back to the ranch," he repeated, in case I hadn't registered his decision. "Maybe those heifers'll come in on their own by the time we get back."

I nodded my agreement. He was in charge of this situation and I trusted him to know what to do.

Tacho led Rose upstream. He brought the boy and his sister, who was wrapped in my poncho, out of the brush.

The girl appeared to be about thirteen years old. Tacho gave the boy his poncho and when he had slipped it on, offered the remainder of his burrito to the two of them, which they eagerly accepted. Taking his time, he shared his canteen. They drank deeply.

When the children were ready, Tacho set the girl lightly onto his saddle and then hoisted the boy up behind her on the horse's withers. Rose shied a little and Tacho whacked her on the side of her head. He led the mare along the canyon floor, passing me and continuing toward the Jeep. I reined Blockhead around and followed.

The girl did not look up as they passed but the boy met my eyes and smiled. He was beautiful.

We retraced our steps to the windmill. We tied our horses to the mesquite tree by the trough and unsaddled them. We hefted our saddles into the back of the Jeep against the unlikely event that anyone should come by while we were gone. People did steal saddles, but we were sure no one would bother the horses while we were away. Blockhead bit and kicked strangers for fun, and Rose would follow his lead.

I offered the rest of my pot roast sandwich to the children but after a glance at Tacho, they shook their heads. Tacho set the wooden toolbox from the front seat into the bed of the Jeep. He drove home. The children rode between us, crouching low for the mile or so on the County Road before we reached the driveway to Headquarters. We saw no other vehicles.

Tacho dropped me at my house and drove the Jeep with the children past the barn toward his home. Sara emerged onto our porch when she heard us, surprised to see us home so early. I told her, and we lingered in the shade of the doorway for a moment, watching.

Sofia came out to meet Tacho when she heard the Jeep. They talked for a moment and then she shepherded the children into their home.

A few minutes passed. Sofia brought my poncho back out to Tacho, who had stayed in the dooryard, leaning against the Jeep, braiding his lariat. She gave him a fresh burrito and he backed the Jeep around and drove back toward our house.

Sara and I slipped into the kitchen to avoid giving the impression we were nosy. When the Jeep pulled into our driveway, I returned to my porch. Tacho stepped out of the Jeep and we shook hands. He gave me a hint of a smile as he stepped around to the right-hand door so I could drive. The toolbox was back in its usual spot on the front seat.

We returned to Box Canyon, saddled our horses and rode upstream. We rousted the heifers out of the brush at the head of the canyon and followed them downstream and into the trailer without incident. The hay proved too tempting for them, and all four squeezed into the trailer.

The boy's footprint was still etched in the sand when we rode upstream. Tacho made a point of guiding Rose along that edge of the streambed to obliterate it. No other sign of the children's presence remained, at least to my tracker's eye.

Tacho asked for Tuesday off; I was glad to comply. Sara and Sofia had talked during the afternoon while the two children slept, safe in Tacho's home.

Sara told me the whole story that evening. The children were indeed Guatemalan. They had come north through Mexico on the roof of a train, and crossed the border with a man who said he was their uncle, along with a dozen other immigrants, late Saturday night, in the midst of a crowd of drunken tourists.

The group hitched a ride in the bed of a pickup as far as a little crossroads town on the back side of the Canciones, when the Border Patrol stopped them and captured four men, including the uncle; everyone else ran into the desert night.

When the group got away from the *migra* and out into the desert wilderness, the *coyote* took an interest in the girl, and the two children fled after the boy confronted the man and was fisted and stripped of his clothes. By this time, the girl had no clothes either.

The two climbed down the cliff at the top of Box Canyon at dawn Sunday morning and no one followed them. The boy found the trough and windmill. He had the idea of waiting until darkness fell on Sunday and then walking out toward the lights of the city in the valley, some forty miles through the desert.

By God's grace it rained and they stayed put. The boy had been on his way to the windmill for water when he encountered the heifers fleeing up the canyon; he also heard us coming and followed suit.

Sofia had learned that the children's parents lived and worked in Omaha. Sara gave Sofia a hundred dollars from the ranch safe to put toward bus tickets; Tacho would drive them into town on Tuesday.

Tacho's two children were at school that Monday. Sofia called her cousin to arrange for her kids to invite their two for the night, as they often did, back and forth. Sofia brought her own children's birth certificates along on Tuesday in case someone on the bus asked to see documents.

Sara related the rest of the plan. Tacho would stay home for the three days it took his wife and the two Guatemalans to get to Omaha, and for Sofia to fly back. Sara put her airline ticket on our credit card.

We weren't sure what Tacho planned to tell his children, and Sara certainly didn't intend to ask.

I listened to the story. I knew the women were as close as Tacho and I were.

"You know," I said when she finished, "this is all against the law. We could all end up in jail for this."

Sara gave me a look identical to the one Tacho had earlier when he called me "*vaquero*."

That was the last anyone ever mentioned the children, but when I happen to catch a glimpse of one of those four heifers, six years old now and profitable cattle for us all, I think of that April morning and the one miraculous footprint still etched in my memory.

I say a prayer of gratitude for rain and sunshine, family and home and all that remains good in the world.

COYOTE MUSIC

Early August: the heart of rainy season.

Sara and I relaxed on the ranch house porch. All afternoon we had watched heavy rain fall on Pastures Three and Twelve. Though the storms were over for the day, occasional thunder still tumbled down from the high peaks behind us. It was time to rest.

The western sky was clearing and the sunset had begun its raucous celebration of cloud and sky and mountain. We settled back in our stretched cowhide chairs to watch the show.

Across the valley, the charcoal mountains leaned against a soft palette streaked with reds and oranges that would have been gaudy in a painting, but somehow found perfection in nature. High above us, night's deep purple blanket got set to unroll leisurely down the sky.

Evening was in no hurry and neither were we. The desert smelled spicy after the rain, and knee-deep new grass drove all memory of drought from the cattle's souls. The last clouds cleared and a waxing crescent moon emerged half-way down the sky. With it, the first tentative coyote yips rose from the draw at the foot of Headquarters.

I took Sara's hand and inhaled slow and deep. For as long as I could remember, we had fallen asleep summer nights lulled by the coyotes' high octave music. It was as much a part of ranch life as postholes and saddle leather and lots easier to love. In a moment, another coyote picked up the tune from the draw and then two more answered from the hill in the horse pasture, a half mile or so past the barn.

Sara leaned toward me. "They're teaching their puppies to howl tonight," she said softly.

"Today I saw the mother and three pups working the grass right below the barn, catching packrats."

"It was amazing," she continued. "They crept through the grass; you wouldn't have known they were there except the tops of the grass twitched a little. All of a sudden the mother would leap up in the air like a dolphin and pounce back down on a packrat. She came up with the rat in her teeth, chewed it a few times and then gave it to the pups. I couldn't see them at first, but I could hear them tussling and growling over it."

"Then the mom would catch another. This went on for an hour or so and I didn't get anything done; I was just leaning on the fence, watching."

Sara laughed softly. "She must have known I was there but she didn't take any notice. I got a good sight of the pups when she led them across the dust bowl where the horses roll, just below the corral."

"It was almost as if she was showing them off to me."

"Coyotes can tell when a person means them no harm," I scootched my chair closer to hers and leaned my shoulder lightly against her. "I'll tell you a funny story. It's about that government guy they sent out here to chase coyotes. I heard it from Tom."

I leaned back in my chair and set the context for the story. "Tom's got that section of Federal land, you know, at the north end of his place. The Feds evidently have a new policy where they want to rid their property of coyotes; probably the sheep lobby working overtime."

"In any event, they sent this dude out from Washington with a pickup and all manner of gear. He came by Tom's last week to ask where the coyotes lived. He'll probably get around to us before the summer's over."

Sara snuggled against me. The evening was starting to cool and the horizon turned plum velvet. We sat silent for a while. Venus sparked to life below the moon, skimming on the sunset's wake. The coyotes were in full song now and bullfrogs had started up in the trough below the house.

"So finish your story!" Sara nudged me playfully. I knew she was hooked.

I picked up where I left off, "Tom feels the same way about coyotes as we do, and he's not about to tell this guy anything useful. But he thought he'd teach him a bit about the West, so he says, 'Let me take you out; it's easier if I show you.'"

"Tom took his Jeep and the Fed followed in his pickup. Tom said the guy had traps, cyanide canisters, and bait made from smoked ham hung in string bags, all shrink-wrapped and boxed and ready to go."

"Tom led him out along that blacktop the government built half-way up the south side of camel's hump. Tom knew some coyotes have their dens in the little caves in the sandstone layer above the road, and they hunt the ridgeline, so he keeps waving out his driver's window to keep the guy's attention focused downhill."

"They stop by the first bridge and Tom lets the guy lug his gear down the rock face into the draw. Tells him the coyotes eat the rattlesnakes in the streambed so he needs to find where the snakes live and set his traps there."

"Meanwhile, Tom looks back up toward the ridge and sees four big coyotes sitting in front of their caves like dogs guarding castles. He swears the coyotes nodded at him and laughed. Then they hung motionless, and if he hadn't known right where they were they would have been invisible, they were so well camouflaged."

"Tom told me the coyotes watched every move that government man made, setting his traps and putting out bait."

It was almost full dark now but I could see Sara's smile white like starlight. She leaned her head on my shoulder. Our coyotes in the draw were quiet for the moment, but the pair on the hill kept up their music, answered far up the mountain behind the ranch house. I heard a great horned owl, not far off, and reflected that what packrats the mama coyote had spared would nourish owlets overnight.

"After the government guy set a few traps in the draw, the two of them scrambled back up to the road. Tom told the guy to drive on west, watching for bridges, and set his baits down in the gullies. He made him a little map. He made sure to mention the rattlesnakes again and told the guy to find them; where they were, the coyotes would not be far behind."

"Tom knows those gullies on that south face of camel's hump will run most every day this time of year and wash the traps down, tripping them; the bait would get eaten by the buzzards. The cyanide was in those little pressurized cylinders so that's a worry; hopefully, they'll get tripped by the storms. In any event, no dogs or kids go down in those gullies. We're all smart about snakes."

"He set the fellow on his way with his poison and his traps. Then he stayed parked by the bridge."

"As soon as the Fed's pickup was out of sight, Tom says the four coyotes came down the trail, went right under the bridge, and one by one that the peed on the traps they guy had set. Then they went back under the bridge and up the hill. One of them stopped and turned back and made eye contact with Tom, and Tom swears he grinned. Tom sure did."

"That's quite a story," Sara laughed. "Did you and Tom get any work done, or were you just swapping coyote tales all day?"

I laughed too. "It's rainy season! The living is easy!"

“So it is.” She untangled herself from my arm and stood up and stretched, showing me a line of white skin between her shirt and jeans. I ran my fingernail softly along it and she shivered. There was just enough light left off the west for me to follow her down the porch. “Let’s get to bed,” she called back to me. “Maybe another good rain tomorrow.”

We did. There was.

FENCE LINE

In the winter, Tacho's uncle Elijah lived in the County Jail. He built fence for us from March until the first snow. Once a heavy drinker, Elijah knew the old adobe jail well; he saw most Sunday dawns through barred windows well into his fifties.

One Saturday night, Elijah shot a hole through the tin ceiling of the Taco House Tavern. The bullet missed the lady and her cowboy in the bed above but scared them white as ghosts when it clanged off an iron pipe above their heads and fell back onto the pillow they shared. They rang the Sheriff with more urgency than usual.

This mistake cost Elijah more than an overnight stay in jail. Sheriff Gant's father gave him a cell for the whole winter that year, a hard detox and a long climb toward sobriety. Old Gant knew a good man when he saw one, though. Elijah fixed everything around the jail, from leaky faucets to Deputies' wives. The two men grew close as they aged.

Years passed and Elijah never touched another drop of alcohol. Gant's father retired to his Barkalounger. His son inherited the office and badge and Elijah came with them. A hard worker, and honest, he needed little in winter to keep him happy and even less in summer. Building fence was his real gift. Outmaneuvering other ranchers as Elijah's relative, Tacho talked him into coming on our payroll year 'round.

Elijah refused to live in the bunkhouse with cowboys when it was too cold to be out on the mountain. Young Gant and I talked at the Fair. For Elijah's winter room and board, the ranch traded the Sheriff's department a side of beef for their annual barbecue.

We kept and fed Elijah's black burro at the ranch, and protected the weathered oak coffin that held his fencing tools from prying cowboy eyes and sticky cowboy fingers. Crafted in Mexico for some long-lost ancestor who disappeared before it could be used, the coffin became a toolbox that was passed down through generations of fence builders. It was just the right length for the long iron crow bars, the two-handled shovel, the sledges, shovels, axe, hatchet and saws; as well as the set of oilcloth-wrapped files Elijah used to keep everything razor sharp.

When spring roundup was over, Tacho and I drove into town to bring him home. Elijah always appeared much happier to see his burro than to see Tacho and me. His greeting to us, year after year, was only *"¿Mi montaña—como es? ¿Como está?"*

Tacho told me that his uncle, the burro and the mountain shared one soul.

We had everything ready for them. Elijah spent one night at Headquarters. At first light, we loaded his oaken toolbox and eight spools of barbed wire, canteens, ponchos and tack for the burro into the back of the Jeep pickup. There was plenty of room left for the burro. Because of his history in the Taco House,

Elijah no longer officially owned guns, but we kept his pistol and holster at the ranch and we put them in the glove box for him until we got up the mountain.

Tacho and I loaded our horses into the trailer. Although Elijah rode between us in the cab coming back from town, he would not sit up front on the range; Tacho told me this was out of respect for us but I suspect it was because the elder preferred the company of his burro. We closed the trailer and returned to the Jeep.

The sunrise lit up the old man like a golden eagle as he balanced on the curled rail of the pickup bed, his hat between his knees, rolling a cigarette with one hand and scratching the burro's neck with the other. They both regarded us without expression as we climbed into the cab. They were already on the mountain in their minds.

Tacho was in high spirits. Compared to Elijah, he was almost garrulous. On the way up the mountain we reviewed the fence lines we had planned for his uncle to build.

"He'll run a line just south of the ridge up to Juniper Flat." Tacho predicted. "That's where he'll set his first corner. He'll leave half the wire there so he can stretch it downhill—the spool weighs better than a hundred pounds and it helps itself."

"He won't bring the burro down from Juniper Flat as long as he's working there. That little *caballo* will get drunk as a *chulu* if he eats too many juniper berries," Tacho's broad smile spread across his face at the thought. "*Tío* won't let him nibble while he's dragging posts. He'll cut some posts, set up his canvas and poncho and sleep there tonight, then tomorrow come down the line marking soft spots."

"The burro'll have the flat to himself. It's been a long winter on hay for both of them. *Tío* might eat a cactus bud or two but he won't share them with the burro. They know each other too well."

"It's berries for the burro!"

Tacho laughed out loud and then brayed softly to imitate the burro. He glanced back through the window toward the bed of the pickup to make sure his uncle hadn't heard him. He returned to the business at hand. "Five miles of fence to build for that government contract. There's plenty of juniper for this side but he'll need some steel posts when he gets over the top. How many we got?"

I had done the calculation and stocked a thousand in November when steel posts were cheap. We'd used a few for a grass enclosure by the river, and I'd welded six end-to-end for a brace when the windmill at Frijole Wells pulled out of its cement footings in a January storm. The permanent fix was next on our list now that roundup was over.

I added up the sides of the grass enclosure in my head. "We've got nine hundred and sixty four left," I concluded.

"OK, *bueno*," Tacho replied. "That's two miles. If he can find a line down the cliff at the top of Sweetwater Canyon he'll have plenty."

I glanced in my side mirror and saw the old man resting easily on the rail of the bed. The road was bumpy but his back and shoulders were set straight and square and he appeared comfortable and unconcerned. In my other mirror I could see the burro standing stolidly in the bed, facing the trailer that rattled behind us. "He knows the line." I responded. "There's not a cliff on this ranch that old man hasn't been up and down a dozen times in his life. I think he sprouts wings and flies when we're not around."

"He doesn't need wings." Tacho said. "He's got that burro. You ever see it walk up a wall? It's like a fly. No horse could ever go where he goes. The two of them, they're family." He thought a minute and smiled again. "My family! *Que Diós me ayuda!"*

We had driven as far as we could. The road petered out at a mesquite corral and a windmill. Dust and manure and cobwebs softened the north wall of the corral like a stucco frieze. The south wall was bright as polished silver.

The fence ended here, too. The ridge rose steep to the east, its knife edge separating daylight from dark. Juniper Flat blanketed the mountain's hip a thousand feet above us. For millennia it had sheltered only deer and the occasional mountain lion that preyed on them. Newly leased Forest Service land, it promised good winter browse for another sixty heifers if we could put a fence around it. Elijah was our man.

Tacho and I unloaded our horses and tightened their cinches. I got our canteens and filled them at the windmill while Tacho helped Elijah pack the burro. The packsaddle rested on a sheepskin pad and a brightly striped saddle blanket. Elijah cinched it tight. It took both of them to set the big oak toolbox lengthwise atop the packsaddle. Tacho hung three sets of saddle bags over the long case and filled these with boxes of spike nails, fencing staples, cans of beans and oil. He strapped a fifty-pound bag of flour on top.

He unfolded a rugged canvas travois and secured the barbed wire spools to its frame, then clipped the shafts to the pack saddle's girth and breastplate.

I gave Elijah his pistol in its holster and he put a box of ammo in another saddlebag. His canteens finished the load. This would be all he needed until July; one season when the rains were good he shot a deer, dried the meat to jerky and went all the way to November without restocking.

Elijah always walked. Tacho and I rode. I took the lead, followed by the old man and his burro dragging the travois. Tacho brought up the rear. I could hear Tacho's Spanish softly drifting uphill as we rode. I imagine he was describing for his uncle what we had in mind.

Elijah said nothing that I could hear, all the way to the top. We climbed through several climates and the cactus told the story.

Near the corral it was all cholla. As we set out up the ridge, prickly pear cacti clustered close by the trail, first big flat green paddles, with buds hinting at their lemon yellow blossoms, then smaller purple prickly pears, with flowers the color of ripe peaches in the sun. Higher, tiny rainbow cactus and bright turquoise pincushions sprung from cracks in the quartz rock of the ridge, their delicate flowers hiding tiny barbed spines. Hedgehog cactus peeked from sheltered nooks where they got more sun than wind.

What soil remained on the steep south face blended subtly from gray toward red the higher we climbed. Hummingbirds defended their territory, startling the horses as they flashed green and gold across the trail. Century plants danced overhead.

If snakes saw us pass, they stayed hidden and quiet.

The ride took close to an hour. The trail grew steep and I reined in my horse to let the burro rest until Elijah's glare prodded me on. All the horses were blowing when we crested the last scree and came into the cool shade of the junipers. We dismounted. A spring moistened the granite at the entrance to the Flat and pooled before disappearing into the scree. Dragonflies hovered up around us and water-striders shot for cover as the horses and burro pushed their noses into the water.

Tacho and Elijah unloaded the burro and travois. They lugged the toolbox a few yards back into the Junipers. Elijah opened the hasps and tipped the top back. He took out his axe and unwrapped the oilcloth that had protected its head from rust all winter, and removed his leather gloves and tested the axe edge with his callused thumb. He smiled and nodded to us.

He said something in Spanish to his burro, removing its saddle and harness and setting them on the tarp.

Tacho collapsed the travois and tied it behind his saddle. There was nothing to keep us, now that we had brought everything up the mountain and reviewed with Elijah the plan for the fence. Nevertheless, Tacho and I lingered. The view of the valley was magnificent, spreading a hundred miles off to the northwest. Cotton fields greened its watercourse far below. A curl of smoke rose from a late branding fire on the ranch across the valley. The sun reflected off big truck windshields on the road to Mexico far below, but no sound reached us except the trickle of water from the spring into the pool and the regular slap of Elijah's axe and hatchet as he began crafting fence posts. The morning air was crystal.

Elijah was the most efficient workman I had ever witnessed, and Tacho and I always savored this first spring outing as an excuse to watch him work for as long as he as he and his burro would endure our presence. He had the whole fence planned in his mind, and set out to select first his corner posts, and then, his line posts from the thick stand of junipers. It took him little time to fell and limb a tree. He sharpened the ends of the thin line posts with his hatchet and squared off the thick corner posts with his saw. Twice during the hour we lingered he stopped to sharpen his axe; once he touched up the angle of the saw, keeping it sharp as a bayonet. The burro dozed, flicking flies with its tail.

When the sun got high, Tacho and I rode back down the mountain. We returned to Headquarters and traded the horse trailer for the cement mixer and spent the rest of that day at Frijole Wells pouring new footings for the windmill. No wind blew, so we got lots done.

Months passed and I seldom thought of Elijah. Tacho dropped more spools of barbed wire at the mesquite corral sometime in late May and they disappeared, so we knew the old man and his burro were still working. A four-strand line of perfectly spaced barbed wire appeared down the south face of the ridge, cornered at the corral. Backpackers or birdwatchers may have come across the two in the high country, but if so we never heard.

Rainy season came late that summer.

Early one Sunday morning, a few days before the solstice, I sat bolt upright in bed in the predawn dark, my eyes wide open and my heart pounding. Sara stirred and I felt the bed shift as she rose on one elbow. Her words were slurred with sleep, "What is it?"

"Elijah's burro! Right there at the foot of the bed!"

"You were dreaming," she murmured, and the bed creaked as she lay back. "Go back to sleep."

I fumbled for the flashlight beside the bed and played its beam across the room. I was wide awake. The room was as always, but I smelled the burro as clearly as if I were in his stall at the barn.

"He was here. I swear it."

"Well if he was he's gone now. Wake me if he comes back with an elephant." Sara burrowed back toward sleep and I turned the flashlight off and sat on the edge of the bed for a few minutes. As my eyes adjusted to the dark I could see the window emerge, a frame of gray at the edge of my vision when I focused on the wall. Otherwise, the room was as dark as the bottom of a mine.

I sighed. No more sleep for me. I slipped into the bathroom, and feeling for the string to the wall fixture on the left of the sink, pulled it in the dark. The bulb flickered, grew bright and steady, then flashed out. Dead quiet on the ranch, too late for owls but not early enough for songbirds, and pitch dark once again. The image of the light burned my eyes, and I blinked a few times and listened to my heart.

The dream had unnerved me, and I leaned on the counter over the sink for a moment in the dark, listening, half convinced I'd hear the burro breathing. I pulled the string to the fixture on the other side of the sink and this time the bulb stayed lit. My half face in the mirror looked back at me with some skepticism, one eye wide open, the other in shadow. What now?

I closed the bathroom door softly and sat on the edge of the tub. Minutes passed and I figured I might as well get started on the day. My jeans and boots were by the bed, so I crept back into my bedroom, gathered them and carried them toward the porch. It seemed as if the smell of the burro still hung in the dark air. I wondered if I should leave Sara alone, but then laughed nervously at my concern. This was no interest of hers.

On the porch no moon shone, but the stars were bright and close and I could see enough to dress in the cool darkness. I went along the porch and into the kitchen, turning on every light and running the water in the sink until it got cold. I drank two glasses and felt better.

I found a clean white shirt hanging over the dryer, and taking my big flashlight from the shelf by the back door, I set out for the barn. Song sparrows had sensed the dawn by now, although it was still an hour away. Their rustling and singing accompanied me.

I slid the barn door open. I don't know exactly what I was looking for, but I didn't find it. A few horses were standing asleep in the corral and the burro's stall was empty and bare. A skunk slipped under the fence, headed home from his night of hunting. A barn cat found me and purred, thinking I had come early to milk.

But it was Sunday and some cowboy's morning to milk. I needed Tacho. I sat on a hay bale by the fence to watch the dawn come, which in its time it did.

Another hot dry day beckoned. I watched Tacho's house for movement, and when I saw his screen door open and his cat slip out, I knew he was up and made my way along the path and knocked lightly.

Tacho's daughter Anita greeted me. She did not seem at all surprised to see me. "Good morning!" she said cheerfully. "Dad's shaving. Mami spent the night in town decorating the church."

I must have looked blank because she smiled and continued, "St. John's Sunday. I guess you don't celebrate it in your church but it's a big deal for us. The rains come, the corn grows; you know, the whole nine yards."

She was home from college a week or so and helping her parents and the rest of us with the ranch work. She had straight white teeth and Tacho's shiny black hair. "Come on in and have a seat," she continued. "I'll tell him you're looking for him."

I took off my hat and sat down at the table. She came back from the hall and set a cup of coffee and plate with a tortilla and honey in front of me. She pulled 'round a chair and sat backwards on it, leaned on the rail and regarded me with a question in her eyes but still the smile. "What's up?"

I'd known her since she was born, and she knew me and my family well. "I thought I saw Elijah's burro in our house last night and it spooked me."

"That mean old beast spooks me in broad daylight," she laughed. "I never turn my back on him. He bites!"

"Where are they this summer?"

"Way up on top, Juniper Flat and higher." I replied. "They're building fence in a big 'Z' over the top and around the backside of the ridge to the mesquite corral in Pasture Eight. For the heifers."

She nodded. We sipped our coffee. In a moment Tacho came out and I stood and shook his hand. His daughter gave him a cup of coffee and we stepped out onto his porch. The sun was nearly up by now, the darkness nearly gone.

"When was the last time you saw Elijah?" I asked him.

"Same as you, back in March. I've seen their tracks at the windmill and he's stretched the first section down to the corral. Built a nice corner there but I imagine he's way up top in this warm weather. Anything the matter?" Tacho met my eyes.

I told him about the burro by my bed and he took me dead serious, nodding as I described its shaggy black pelt and its big shiny eye rolling at me. And the smell.

"Sure." Tacho said. "That makes sense. If we were in Iowa and on TV it'd be Lassie. Probably not good news, though. Let's take a ride up there."

"What about church?" I asked.

"They can handle it." He smiled and with a slight chin motion indicated the dawn spreading up the valley before us. "This is my church. Yours, too. Whatever we find on that mountain is up to us to deal with. Maybe it was just a nightmare."

I could see he was humoring me. He knew as well as I did what we would find.

We went back in and I finished my tortilla. Tacho's wife Sofia kept bees and the honey was divine. His daughter took my coffee cup and rinsed it and set it in on the drain board. She was dressed in white and looked very clean and pretty. She was not upset to learn that she would be driving to town alone to meet her mother. She headed out in Tacho's pickup, and I swung by home and spent a few minutes with Sara in the kitchen. She was skimming the cream off the fresh milk the cowboy had brought. I told her Tacho and I would be back by noon. He and I met back at the barn; he had saddled and loaded our horses and we set out in the Jeep with the trailer behind.

It was a quiet ride up the ridge. We found Elijah in the shade beneath his canvas tarp, wrapped in his poncho. His barefoot body was already stiff but no flies had gathered yet. His fine old boots were set side by side, socks tucked in to keep scorpions out.

We lifted him gently, still wrapped in the bright poncho, into his oak toolchest. His shovels were sharp and the red soil was soft among the Junipers. We dug six feet down, set the coffin in the grave and gently filled it. I grimaced at the thump of the first few shovelfuls falling on the oak, but soon the swish of soil piling on soil was the only sound. Tacho squared a manzanita cross with some rawhide from his lariat.

We said a prayer. It appeared Elijah's last act had been to shoot his burro, probably at sunset the evening before, looking west over the valley, right before he removed his boots and socks, rolled himself snug in his poncho, and lay down in his shelter. The burro had dropped right down with no pain, a clean finish to its long life.

No one buried burros.

How Elijah knew it was his time we could not guess. He left no sign. His tools were laid out in order on the granite by the spring at the top of the scree, where he knew we would find them. No rust clouded their gleam. He knew we would come soon, and that they would be safe.

Tacho said another prayer in Spanish over the burro, now just a sack of bones, his gray lip curling back to reveal his old yellow teeth. I threw a few Juniper branches over him.

Tacho walked down the mountain, leading his horse laden with the old man's tools strapped to his saddle with his lariat, covered with Elijah's tarp and empty canteens. I rode behind, thinking about the burro in my dream, wondering who I could get to finish the fence Elijah had begun.

It rained hard that night with lots of lightning. One of our mares foaled just before midnight and I named the colt Johnny. He's a four-year-old now, well broke and smart enough to smell rain a day off. On his birthday, I rode him up along the fence line all the way to Juniper Flat. Johnny drank from the spring near the burro's bones, which lay untouched on the red earth, white as cotton, and soft as the solstice night air.

BAD COWBOY

My Chicago brother-in-law and I set out for a ride one Sunday morning to give our wives some peace from our political wrangling. I was on Mitch and he rode Zipper, the closest we have to a Thoroughbred.

We escaped Headquarters Pasture and wound up the trail toward the saddle. As we neared the summit, the trail was steep and gravelly. It became a sandstone staircase, smoothed by millennia of wind and water and the passage of deer seeking water in the canyon beyond. We never brought cattle over this trail, but it was fine for horses, a shortcut with magnificent scenery.

We stopped at the top to let the horses catch their breath. There was plenty of room to stand side by side, and Rob reined Zipper up alongside Mitch. The two horses touched noses, and we sat them admiring the view.

Sawtooth Canyon lay before us dressed in her spring finery. Yellow poppies and pink huahija lined the mountain rivulets that fed the canyon. Although it was at least 80 degrees in the sun where we rested, a few deep slashes of snow still sparkled on the high peaks. A gentle south wind brought the music of flowing water from the canyon far below.

Mitch and Zipper pricked their ears, but it was not the water music that caught their attention. Rob and I followed their gaze and saw a shiny turquoise pickup winding along the trail in the valley floor. After a few moments, we could hear its laboring engine and an occasional clank as it bottomed out on a rock. The road was a challenge for a Jeep, and this pickup lacked the clearance. Puffs of dust rose from time to time as it spun its tires, but still it pressed on.

Rob gave me an inquiring glance. "That's JR's truck," I said. "And he's up to no good, you can bet."

"JR?" Rob questioned me. "Do I know this person?"

"Probably not. He's one of the cowboys; lives in the bunkhouse and keeps his horse in a steel corral across the yard from the rest. You've probably heard his horse whinnying at night. He's a gelding but Tacho doesn't think they got it all, and he's hell on the other horses; bothers the mares and fights with the geldings. Name's Geronimo—-hell of a name for a cow horse—but that's the least of what we've got with JR."

Rob raised one eyebrow. "Why don't you just fire him? It seems like you've got plenty of reasons, not that you need any in this state."

"Well, I would," I allowed, "but I found out from Tom when I ran into him at the Cattle Grower's meeting that JR had worked for him, stole from him, and he fired the bastard. Then things started to happen at Tom's ranch: cut fences, salt blocks in the well, a calf with its hammies slit and left for the javelinas; nothing he could pin on JR but he knows that's who's been doing it.

Rob appraised the distant pickup as if it were a tick crawling up his arm. "It would have been nice to have known this before you hired him. He didn't give you references?"

I laughed but without much humor. "Right. Show me a cowboy who has references and I'll show you a born liar. They're a breed of their own—no past, no future—you have to take them on a handshake. Most of them are okay. Tacho and I have three rules: no drinking on weeknights, no automatic pistols, and if you steal something bigger than a Prince Albert can, you're gone."

"That covers expensive stuff like fencing pliers and horse trailers; they all believe they have the right to take small stuff. It's part of the business. We've actually done pretty well over the years. But this JR, he's a problem. There's stuff at the well that he could sell at the flea market today in town and we'd never be the wiser."

"Maybe we'd better get down there and stop him." Rob suggested.

"No, he's a smart SOB and he'll see us on the trail; it's wide open and as soon as we're moving he'll catch sight of us. Cowboys train their eyes to catch movement and it's the one thing he's good at."

"He won't see us if we stay right here against the south face behind us," I nodded at the sandstone. "The horses are the right color and for once you aren't wearing red. Ninety percent of his attention's got to be on that road."

"He's just the kind to have a turquoise Ford," I mused. "He wears that felt Stetson all summer."

"So what are we going to do?" Rob asked. "Just watch while he robs you blind? Shouldn't we go back to the ranch and call the Sheriff?"

"No, that won't help. Even if the Sheriff caught him on his way into town and I pressed charges, he'd beat it and carry a grudge. You're a Chicago lawyer, Rob, you know how that works." I smiled at him; despite our differences, we were good friends and had shared lots over the years.

"I've got to figure out a way to get him to quit of his own accord."

"Tell me everything you know about this guy." Rob mused, now keenly interested in my dilemma. I suddenly felt lots better about the day. Rob never lost.

"Well, he hates sheep," I said, "as most cowboys do. But he takes it to an extreme. He won't even set at a roundup fire if we've got lamb stew bubbling on it. Gets up and spits and walks away."

"That's attractive," Rob put in.

"And he's a real race-baiter. You know Tacho has Yaqui blood, and he calls him 'Joe,' which is a slur. The other cowboys give him a wide berth. No one really cares for him but he doesn't seem to notice."

"Cowboys are an independent breed; they keep their own counsel."

"But none would be sorry to see him go, you're telling me?"

"Right."

"Does he have any quirks we could take advantage of?"

I could tell Rob was thinking like a big city prosecutor and that pleased me. I thought for a few minutes myself, and began to enjoy the day again despite JR's intrusion into our ride.

Our horses hung motionless beneath us except for an occasional swish of their tails or ears. They had lost interest in the pickup. I liked to imagine that Mitch and Zipper enjoyed a Sunday ride in springtime as much as we did; a day off from herding cattle or struggling along a fence line where the footing was edgy. Although they still carried us on their backs, I imagined that at some level they felt good toward Rob and me. These two, our favorites, never tried to bite or kick us, and when we loosened their reins they loved to run with the wind on the flats, bits in their teeth.

Zipper always outran Mitch but Mitch gave it all his heart every time. He wanted to win for me, too.

We watched the turquoise truck slip from sight into the mesquite grove that cradled the well. After a few minutes, I came up with a response to Rob's question. "Well, JR's superstitious as all get out. Most cowboys are a little superstitious; it takes luck to survive in this business, but JR carries it to an extreme. Rabbit's foots, horseshoes over every door, and he's death on numbers. He shoots craps with the other cowboys every chance he gets, and he always talks numbers."

"The worst for him is 666. Tacho told me JR claims it's something from the Bible, but he must be reading a different Bible from mine. I never heard of it."

"It's the number of the 'Beast'" Rob said. "Some fundamentalist sects think it symbolizes the anti-Christ." He thought for a moment.

"OK," he said. "I've got your solution. You'll need to get the rest of the hands in on it, or at least Tacho, but that shouldn't be too hard from what you've told me."

I was eager to hear what Rob had in mind, "Tell me more."

"OK. Orthodox Easter is two weeks from today. My brother's wife is Armenian, and they eat lamb for Easter—"

"So do we." I interjected.

"Not like they do. I'm talking a whole lamb, cooked on a spit. They live west of the city and her whole family, dozens of them, get together and have a great big party, starting at midnight Saturday. They dance and sing and cook a lamb or two and then feast. It's the best Easter you could imagine. Beats our Presbyterian nosh all to hell."

I could tell he was showing off his appreciation of the new multiculturalism, and ribbing me too, but I didn't take the bait.

"I'm listening. Tell me more."

"Step one: we get the word out through our wives and Tacho's wife that my brother and his wife are flying out here to join us all for Easter."

He saw my expression "They aren't, of course," he hurried to reassure me.

He'd respected the look I'd given him. The only time his brother had been on the ranch, for some cousin's wedding a few years back, he'd mistaken a roll of number six weave for chicken wire and been dumb enough to open his mouth about it. We'd laughed: Rob's brother was a dude. Tacho brought up his gaffe whenever Rob's annual visit came around. Tacho had known his share of dudes. He knew Chicago lawyers, too, from the stockyard side of town.

Rob went on, "But we get the rumor started. By the time it reaches your perp, it'll be fact. And we include my sister's family's penchant for Easter lamb, whole lamb."

"Step two, you start to plan the party. You get the other cowboys to pretend to dig a pit in the sandy draw below the house. You talk about the lamb. You need the lamb. Put the news out through the women."

Rob warmed to his topic, "Here's where our friend JR comes in. He knows, like we all do, that the nearest live sheep are up on the Reservation, along Route 666."

"Step three, tell him—don't ask him!—to go up in his pickup and bring a lamb back. Tell him it has to be alive, because killing the lamb is part of the ceremony. That'll freak him out before he even hears the rest of your instructions."

"Then tell him he needs to bring the lamb back in the cab of his pickup! It can't be harmed in any way; can't get what they call a 'blemish.' No bruises or scratches from bouncing around in the back of the pickup all the way back from the Reservation."

"Be nonchalant about it as if it's something you do every year," Rob went on. "Be sure you specify the route number several times when you're telling him how to get there."

"You're the boss. Set him up by telling the other hands not to do anything for JR; do something to your Jeep so he can't drive it, you and Tacho know lots about engines."

He thought a little more and pulled a stalk of last year's grama grass out of its tube on the cliff beside the trail, and nibbled on its sweet tip as though it were a peppermint cane from a Christmas tree. I waited, watching his face. A slow smile crept across it, like a bobcat ready to pounce on an unsuspecting vole.

"Step four, give the other cowboys a few days off right before Easter. They probably have families somewhere; make up an excuse. Tacho and his wife can know the whole plan, they'll get a kick out of it. Tacho would never loan his pickup to his best friend, never mind some low-life *vaquero*, but you can bet this JR'll ask for it at the last minute."

"You can count on this: JR won't tell you no to your face. It'd harm his cowboy pride. But he'll quit before he'll do this job. Money in the bank."

"I can see why they pay you those big bucks," I smiled back. Rob was a good man to have on your side. "It's worth a try."

We went home by a different route, cutting along a deer trail through the basin above Headquarters, and then down past the Hot Springs. We enjoyed our Sunday.

Monday morning, when Tacho and I met, I implemented Rob's plan. It worked. Way before sunrise on Good Friday morning JR drove off in his turquoise pickup with his cut mustang in his horsetrailer.

That was three years back, and we haven't seen or heard from him since.

Tom's problems ended, too. He buys Rob and me a big Chicago Pizza at the County Fair each spring when Rob visits, to thank us for ridding the county, and perhaps the whole state, of that bad cowboy.

SHOE LOOSE

Tacho the horseman squatted in the deep shade north of the barn. Except for the smooth rhythmic motions of his fingers as he braided a rawhide lariat, his body was as straight and still as the live oak tree in the center of the barnyard.

Tacho's eyes, onyx bright in the even deeper shade under his hat brim, followed a cowboy shoeing a bay mare beside the tree.

He watched the cowboy remove the old shoes one by one; trim and file the hooves; then, as the afternoon waned and the shadows lengthened, forge four new shoes with fire and anvil. One by one, he nailed them in place.

The mare was gentle and well-broke, and gave the cowboy no trouble beyond resting as much weight as she could on whichever hoof he held aloft.

The men did not speak. When the cowboy finished his work, he led the mare to the barn. Tacho stood and stretched as they drew close; he stood a head taller than the cowboy.

In response to a gesture from Tacho that would have been imperceptible to someone unfamiliar with horses, both the cowboy and the mare drew up six feet short of the tall man.

They stood at ease as Tacho lifted each hoof. He began with the left foreleg; then he stepped beneath the mare's chin and checked the right. Back under her neck again, Tacho ran his hand along her withers and gently down her left flank. She lifted her left rear hoof obligingly and he cradled it against his thigh for a moment, set it gently down, and passing once more beneath her neck, repeated the sequence on her right side.

Where each shoe joined its hoof, the tall horseman slid his calloused forefinger carefully along the line. All the while he spoke softly in Spanish to the horse, but said nothing to the cowboy. Then he let them proceed.

Two months passed.

The sun was considerably higher in the sky and spring buds were swollen on the cactus. Tacho and I followed the track of a cow and calf along a dusty draw in a pasture ten miles from Headquarters and four miles from our horse trailer. We had followed these tracks all the way from water, where we'd rousted four buzzards from a fresh afterbirth.

We were both surprised the cow had not eaten it, and that she and her calf were gone. Something was amiss.

Tacho had been first to notice the thin scratch line the cow's track left on the dust where no wind had disturbed it. Dragging her left hind leg; not bad yet, but it never got better. And we found no place where the pair had stopped and stood still so the calf could nurse.

"What you got?" Tacho asked me.

"No clue," I mused. "I've never seen a cow lead a newborn so far when there's nothing after them; they were right at water. What's she thinking?"

"Wishing she was a horse!" Tacho replied with a smile. "That's all cows think."

We'd had this conversation maybe a hundred times. It passed the time when the two of us rode herd. His line was my cue to threaten to bring sheep on the place, which would lead to one of his infinite supply of sheep stories from his wife's aunt, who was a deputy on the Reservation.

The stories all ended with the same moral: if God had created an animal dumber than the cow, it was the sheep.

Horses, on the other hand, were considerably higher than humans on Tacho's pantheon of creation.

Today, our script never got that far. As we traversed a patch of caliche clay, hard and hot as asphalt at the height of dry season, Tacho suddenly held out his hand toward me. Both horses stopped still.

"Ride on up there a bit, " Tacho advised me. "Let me watch her gait a second."

I hadn't felt anything, but I urged the mare forward and she walked on across the caliche and onto the trail the cattle had cut through the burro weed. I sensed Tacho following about twenty feet back; I kept my eyes on the cow-calf tracks, detecting a little waver. Something was definitely amiss with this cow. An idea began to form in my mind.

"OK, I got it," Tacho called and I reined in so he could come up alongside. "She's dropping her hip; get down a second and I'll take a look."

I complied, careful where I stepped. Although we hadn't seen a snake yet this spring, at this altitude it was warm enough and they'd be irritable as they emerged from hibernation. None was apparent, so I stepped forward and held my mare's head while Tacho talked quietly to her a moment, and then slid his hand down her flank.

The mare picked up her hoof and Tacho cradled her fetlock on his thigh. He had his hook knife out and carefully pried the clods of caked mud from the frog of her hoof. He tapped the heel of the knife lightly along the horseshoe. I felt the mare shiver slightly; she rippled the skin on her flank as if to shoo a fly.

"Fooled me," Tacho muttered. "Good for him, bad for her, bad for him when we get home."

"Here, take a look," he called me back. I dropped the mare's reins straight down; she was trained to stand still, as Tacho's horse was doing.

"Run your finger along here," Tacho indicated the top of the shoe on the outside of her hoof.

I complied.

"Feel anything?"

"No, I don't think so," I responded. "What am I looking for?"

"Do it with your eyes closed," he advised. "Listen inside your head. Feel it?"

"There's like a little ripple, right there," I opened my eyes and pointed to the shoe. "I didn't feel it before but with my eyes closed somehow it showed up.

Tacho nodded. "It's what my dad used to say, 'When you shut off the light to your eye, one comes on in your finger.' Our brains can only handle so much: we're lookers, not feelers."

"I wonder if I could have caught it?" he mused. "No way to know now; the damage is done. *Compadre*, you have a little walk ahead of you."

"OK," I nodded. "But you got to tell me what's wrong. There's a sick cow up there," I motioned to the trail ahead, "and if we don't get to her the calf'll be dead."

"Ok, *bueno*," he replied. "That's a grand. But you got twenty six hundred in horseflesh here and if she puts your weight on that shoe another mile she's shot. Look at that swollen heel!"

"She'll walk as far as she needs to without you on her; she knows how to care for her foot but she'd please you first. If you walk her back to the trailer, she'll be fine. I'll fix her shoe when we get home."

"After you fire that *cabrón* with the anvil," he finished.

"I heard you," I reminded him. "I'm walking! But you've got to tell me what you know about that shoe and how you know it!"

"If you tell me that I'll tell you what's happening with the cow, and you can catch up to her and fix it and we all win," I tempted him.

Tacho took off his hat and wiped his brow with his sleeve as if considering a monumental wager. He raised one eyebrow and looked appraisingly at the mare's hoof, them back to me.

After a moment he replaced his hat, held out his hand and we shook. "Deal," he said. "I go first."

"Fine by me."

Tacho turned his attention to the mare. "When the farrier shapes the shoe the iron has to be just the right temp," he began. "Too cold, it springs and won't hold the curl. Too hot, it doesn't bend smooth; it compresses where he hits it. It's easy to see it when it happens if you're the guy with the hammer: the shoe's orange hot, just starting to fade, and it turns black where you hit it wrong because the heat doesn't run smooth there."

"He knew it soon as he did it, that's what ticks me off." Tacho scowled at the thought of the distant cowboy. "But he went ahead with the shoe. He was in a rush and he thought it might be okay."

"But it wasn't and here we are."

"He'll deny it and give you all kind of lip but that's what happened."

"When the shoe gets on the horse it's not quite smooth right there," the horseman continued, tapping the offending shoe with his forefinger. "That little ripple from the missed strike is either on the bottom where the shoe hits the ground or the top where it meets her hoof."

"If it's on the bottom and the horse never goes on rocks or hardpan, or if you put a rubber base on it like we did in the army when the Calvary was going on cobblestones, you can get away with it. The horse feels it but it doesn't hurt; kind of like a ring on your finger."

"But if it's where the shoe meets the hoof, after a while it starts to hurt because that place on the hoof is carrying a little more than its share of the weight."

"Like an ingrown toenail in a tight boot."

Tacho cast an appraising look at my boots and I could see he was gauging how they fit, knowing I had a walk ahead of me. He seemed satisfied.

"She's not lame yet, and there's no harm done, so we don't have to shoot your cowboy," Tacho gave me that dead serious look he reserved for scaring dudes; and then his face softened to a smile again, "and technically it's my fault, too, 'cause I watched him do it and I didn't catch the ripple on the inside when I checked his work."

"See how her heel bulb is a little swollen? That's why she's dropping her hip. It's touching the ground with your weight on her back. Without you, she'll be fine for those few miles," he nodded in the general direction of water.

"*Lo siento, mi linda*," he murmured in the horse's ear. She swished her tail and tossed her nose and I could've sworn she understood every word.

He tipped his head back in my direction, "I felt something in here," he tapped his own temple, "but I put it aside because I liked the guy and he does know his stuff."

"But now, we got to check every horse he's put a shoe on for the last two months; won't that be fun!"

"The lazy son of a bitch," Tacho snapped.

"OK, *bueno*, I hope I got you angry now, enough to fire him," Tacho laughed. He set the mare's hoof gently on a soft sandy patch, "Your turn."

I returned his smile. My mare had her hoof cocked; her eyelids drooped, napping while we talked.

"Now, my friend," I replied. "I've diagnosed that cow and she's not even here."

He raised one eyebrow; I let the suspense build a few seconds.

"She's got an ascending neuropathy."

Tacho laughed. "In English or Spanish only, *por favor*. I don't speak whatever language you're using."

"Pinched nerve, getting worse."

He nodded and I continued.

"Somehow when she was calving something didn't quite fit; the calf came out all right, and it's strong; we can see that by the fact that it's still trailing along behind her, trying to get a drink."

"But some nerve got pinched inside the cow, in her pelvis or back. I used to know its name, something Latin, but I can't remember it; doesn't matter, anyway."

"Her leg's getting numb. She keeps moving, but she's dragging that one foot, worse all the time."

"Now she's staggering a little. You can see by the track. That's what tipped me off."

"Why does she keep going?" Tacho pressed me. "Why not just stop and rest?

I thought for a minute and gave him my opinion, "The same nerve that's making her leg numb is snapping her like a switch on the back each time she moves. She feels like she's being driven from behind. It probably started when the calf dropped; that's why she didn't even stick around and eat the sack."

"So what do I do when I find her? Nerve surgery?"

I gave him a grim smile. "It's hard to say until you see her. Maybe she's got a prolapsed uterus; you know, where the cow keeps pushing after the calf and the sack comes out and her gut turns inside out?"

Tacho nodded. We'd seen some of these; the biggest problem was they got sunburned if we didn't get them pushed back in soon enough.

"Hope not," he said.

"Me too. Whatever you find, you got to get her to stop and stand still. Once she does, the lashing she's feeling on her backside might stop. Then, she'll relax and let the calf nurse. Best case, the pressure on that nerve settles and she starts to feel her leg. That way you save them both, get her settled down, leave them alone and pretty soon she heals."

"Worst case, well, save the calf if you can," I advised him.

"Pretty good diagnosis, boss!"

This was high praise from Tacho. "I'll catch up with her quick as I can; you head back," he added. "If you get to the trailer first, go ahead home; I'll come back to the water and wait there. If you can't get back, send someone with the trailer. I got water and a burrito."

We shook hands and he swung into his saddle and soon disappeared along the track. My mare pricked up her ears, shook her head and nickered once after them but made no effort to follow.

I took her reins and we started walking, back the way we had come.

It was a new experience for me to see the low desert from the perspective of a pedestrian. I was almost never off my horse at this elevation; we even doctored cattle from horseback, smearing iodine on barbed wire wounds with a long folding swab stick, or roping the cow and holding her still from our horses while some cowboy got down and tended to her in one way or another.

I had never been here afoot alone. Everything looked different. My horizon was much more limited than it was three feet higher on a horse's back.

I kept my eyes on the trail. I began to notice small creatures that were invisible from on high: horned lizards, dung beetles, tiny wasps circling tiny dens in the sand. When we crossed dry arroyos where water had not flowed since August, I glimpsed small powder blue butterflies clustered in dark shady patches, somehow drawing moisture from the parched sand.

I could peer straight into teddy bear chollas where cactus wrens rested on their nests. I became aware of a multitude of tiny sounds. I listened for rattlesnakes.

After about a mile, it hit me that this was the view my horse always had. I turned to her and said out loud, "Let me know if you see something I should!"

She flicked her ear once and continued to plod along. She could have been sleep walking.

"What would Tacho say to her?" I wondered. I realized he kept up a conversation with his mount whenever he wasn't talking to me, speaking so softly I never picked up a word, his lips scarcely moving. I decided to try his technique.

"Do you see any snakes?" I murmured. No response.

"I hope your hip feels okay," I tried. Her eyelids drooped even further.

Maybe she only spoke Spanish. I tried to remember her name, failed. Gave up.

We trudged on. It was very quiet. I began to notice how the soil color shaded subtly from red through orange to tan as the trail wound through the desert; the underbrush evolved as well, in sequence. It all fit.

From the back of a horse the pasture had seemed flat; now that I was walking, I realized that it rolled gently like the muscled back of some huge creature.

I began to imagine the occasional arroyos we crossed as wrinkles in this creature's skin.

From time to time, cows and calves stood on or near the trail. They moved aside when they saw the horse. After another hour or so, I sought the slender shade of a tall sahuaro and stopped to rest. I drank deeply from my canteen. The day was not hot but very dry and the cool water tasted sharp and sweet as tin.

My mare stood patiently in the sun while I rested. I guessed we were more than half way back to our trailer by the water trough. I wondered if she was thirsty. I wondered how Tacho was doing and where he was. I missed him.

We continued. A ways ahead, the skeleton of a long-dead tree arched above the scrub mesquite. It was a landmark in the pasture; the trail forked near its base, one fork leading back to the water, the other to a gate a few miles further. I knew the pasture well and yet I began to doubt my memory. Which fork must I follow?

A lone buzzard perched in the dead tree. Surely it would take wing before we came too close. It did not. I felt its cold gaze as we drew nearer.

"You're nuts!" I thought to myself. "You've ridden this trail a hundred times. It's just a bird, it means nothing. Walk on by."

I forced myself to watch the trail, winding, shimmering, dusty. I scanned the dust, seeking our tracks, lost now in the jumble of cloven hoof prints. I did not look at the tree.

We came to the fork.

I stopped. My mare came up behind and nudged me hard with her nose and forehead. I stumbled aside and she walked right by me, taking the right fork. I scrambled to get back in front of her, to lead her.

When I looked back at the tree the buzzard was gone.

Another hour of walking brought us to the water trough. I let the mare drink while I slipped her saddle off and hoisted it into the back of the Jeep. I was about to load her into the trailer when I heard a horse in the distance.

Soon Tacho came into sight, riding at a brisk trot, easy in the saddle.

"How'd it go? I called to him as he drew up at the trough.

"Good," he shouted. "I caught them at the corner. The cow was pacing the fence; just like you said, she kept flinching like she'd been hit."

Tacho dismounted and let his horse drink. He walked over to us. "I roped her and snared her tight to the corner post,"

"The calf was about done for but when the cow got still he started to suck and pretty soon his tail was going. The old girl twitched but she stood and let him suck, and then after a bit she went to licking him."

"He had stains on his face still; she hadn't cleaned him up and he was pretty dry, but she worked on him with her tongue for a while and he came clean."

"We watched them for a half hour or so. She wasn't worried about us; she got going on the calf and he was all she thought about."

"I couldn't see any tear or anything," he went on. "You could tell she'd just calved but she'd tightened up OK."

"After a bit, she stopped twitching and then she looked at us, and I thought, 'maybe she needs to get back to water.'"

"So I crossed the fence and loosed the rope, and she just stood there for a bit while he sucked; then she set out up the fence, east; you know, there's that windmill at the other corner, closer than here."

"They looked okay so I rode back. How'd you do?"

"Fine," I replied. "I'm glad it isn't August."

"Cows don't calve in August!" Tacho laughed. "It all fits, you know. How're your feet?" He gave my boots his look of critical appraisal.

"Fine. Let's go. We've got work to do."

We loaded the horses and drove back to Headquarters. I got cash out of the safe in my office, found the cowboy by the bunkhouse, paid him his due and fired him. I told him why. He loaded his saddle and his tools and drove off.

Tacho took care of the horses.

FALSE WITNESS

Drought plagued the ranch.

By day, the cowboys hauled water in a steel tank pieced together within the bed of the cattle truck. The water weighed far more than the cattle the truck was designed to carry, so Tacho spent whatever cool hours the nights afforded crafting overload springs and welding their heavy mounts to the truck's frame.

Even so, the cowboys dared not drive the top-heavy truck too fast. It crawled up canyons and groaned through desert arroyos to far-flung water stations. Empty troughs surrounded the wells, their windmills clattering dry sucker rods deep within the well casings. As soon as the cowboys reached the troughs and pumped their cargo of water, desperate cattle swarmed round and drank the troughs dry almost before the lightened truck could leave for Headquarters to reload.

In the lower pastures no good grass remained and dust storms stung every inch of bare skin. Even when the cattle got water, their hides hung like stiff stained parchment on their skeletons.

Some cows followed shade around trees as the days waxed and waned, stepping painfully as if they feared their skin and bones might crumble. Others gave up following shade altogether and bloated and died far from water.

It was all the cowboys could do to pump and haul. They had no time to get out on horseback to seek those cows who wandered too far or became too disoriented from dehydration to come to the tanks.

Circling buzzards alerted us as to their final resting places.

If we were lucky, we managed to find their calves and bring them to Headquarters, our crop for the whole year, all weaned before their time. We fed them milk replacer and what hay we could buy at a premium from northern states the drought had not yet claimed.

In the midst of this drought, lightning roared from the high rainless clouds and sparked forest fires in the Canciones, closing off our higher pastures; we all took days from hauling water to push cattle down into the hot valley.

Throughout July, the fires spread and joined until a third of the mountain range was ablaze.

At the height of the drought Nora arrived.

Our daughter Andrea had met her during summer session at Cornell. I remember her first call home after they met; she was so excited to have found another ranch girl.

"Dad, she knows how it is!" she exclaimed, her voice crackling across the continent. "She can help us! Can she come in August when session's over?"

Hospitality trumped exhaustion and we agreed to the visit. We drove into town late one Saturday to meet their plane. The Canciones shrunk like a shattered jack-o-lantern in our rearview mirror as we left the ranch behind.

The acrid smoke still permeated the night air.

We found the airport nearly deserted in the midsummer heat. Sara and I greeted the girls and they threw their backpacks into the car trunk and slipped into the backseat. Sara tried a few gambits of conversation without much response. "Must be tired," I thought to myself. We headed for home, the rivers of flames flowing up the mountain a macabre beacon for us. After an hour, we reached the foothills and drove into the thick smoke. The red-tinged night swallowed the car and us inside it.

When we got home, Nora and Andrea, not so tired after all, stayed up late talking on the porch. Sara and I fell into bed.

The two girls slept late the next morning. Because it was Sunday, Sara and I did the chores so Tacho and the cowboys could get a break. We did not haul water that day, but planned the cowboys' routes for Monday.

Andrea emerged from the house and stuck to her new friend like thistledown as Nora, a wraith in the smoke, explored the barn and barnyard. The newcomer watched Sara and me at our work but did not engage our labor, keeping her distance, not getting in the way. I wished for Andrea's help, but I did not want to push too hard. "Adjusting to home," I thought to myself and got on with my day. The two left the table soon after supper and retreated to Andrea's room.

Monday morning they slept late again. Stifling my growing resentment, I left the house before they appeared.

When I got to the barn the cattle truck wouldn't start. Tacho tried the usual remedies for vapor lock or fouled plugs, but to no avail. He drained the gas tank and discovered that water had somehow found its way into the fuel. While the cowboys paced nervously, Tacho removed and cleaned and replaced the spark plugs and replenished the gas tank with fresh fuel; but still the engine would not catch.

The cowboys and I left Tacho pondering the truck and wrestled a half dozen rusty 55-gallon drums into the Jeep Pickup. The three cowboys filled these with water and set off for the most critical pastures. Because the pump was wedged into the cattle truck, they planned to tip the heavy barrels into the troughs.

I worried the cement troughs would break when the heavy barrels hit but it was our only option.

At midmorning, Andrea and Sara appeared at the barn without Nora. The three of us dragged sacks of milk replacer from the feed room to begin the laborious task of mixing formula and filling bottles for the calves.

Meanwhile, Tacho dug deeper into the truck's engine.

My daughter and wife worked methodically with the calves and the bottles; Andrea looked exhausted and Sara said little. I returned to the house and tinkered with the radio in the cool pantry, seeking news of rain or fire. From time to time government airplanes lumbered overhead, hidden in the smoke, dropping water on the blackened Canciones.

I nursed my anger at the drought and the smoke and the hot day.

At noon, Tacho knocked at the kitchen door. I emerged from the pantry to meet him. Nora had finally appeared and was huddled over a cup of coffee at the kitchen table. Andrea and Sara were still at the barn nursing calves.

Tacho did not come in. He raised an eyebrow when he saw Nora and motioned me out onto the porch. We stood in the shade, our backs to the house.

"We've got a problem," Tacho began. He cast a glance over his shoulder toward the screen door. "You have a guest?"

"Yeah, a friend of Andrea's. Grew up on ranch but you'd never know it from what we've seen so far," I replied.

I was worried about the truck. Tacho's Army experience had given him an intimate knowledge of truck engines and I'd never seen him stymied. He almost always appeared cool and at ease. But today, his denim shirt was soaked with sweat, his hands were covered with rust and grease, his knuckles raw. For the first time in years I felt genuine fear.

With another glance into the kitchen, Tacho spoke softly, "Let's go over to your office."

I raised my eyebrows. This was unusual. I followed Tacho across the driveway and unlocked the door to the ranch office, a small alcove set in the corner of an adobe outbuilding that housed the shop and backed up to the bunkhouse. We stepped inside and Tacho closed the door behind us.

He dug his forefinger into the watch pocket of his Levi's and extracted a couple of pieces of shiny metal, rolled them with his thumb and forefinger and then set them on my desk. "Here's why that engine won't start."

I gave him a quizzical look. I picked up one of the shiny metal spheres. It was slightly smaller than a copper

BB, but silver. It looked like a ball bearing, the kind you'd find deep in the guts of a front wheel hub. I said as much.

"Exactly," Tacho replied. "Hardened steel, harder than anything inside an engine. But that's where I found them."

"The whole engine's shot," he continued. "God knows how these guys got into the cylinders. When the pistons came up to TDC these wouldn't compress. They're harder than the head so they either cracked the piston or blew out one of the valve seals, breaking the lifter while they're at it; in a couple of places the head gasket was blown, too."

"These balls had to go somewhere when the engine cranked. It only took a couple of seconds--once that crankshaft made a full revolution, all the cylinders were ruined and that engine would never start. There's a bunch of these little guys, everywhere; some got out into the exhaust manifold but most of them are still in the cylinders."

"I can suck them out with the shop vac, but then I've got to rebuild the top half of the engine, maybe the whole engine if I can't save the pistons that're scored. Only other option, maybe better, is a whole new motor."

My heart sank. I know some engine basics so I followed what Tacho was saying. The cattle truck was the lynchpin to the whole water hauling effort. Without it, hundreds of cows and calves would die. "How long?" I asked him.

Tacho sighed, took his white handkerchief from his back pocket and mopped his brow.

"Let's think a minute," he changed the subject. "I can get the balls out, but how'd they get into that engine in the first place? While we're at it, how'd water get into the gas tank?"

"Someone put them there," he concluded.

Tacho saw my expression. I started to speak but he held up his hand to stop me.

I nodded and he continued, "Engines are very simple: fuel, air, compression, spark. That's all that can go wrong. Only a few things are impossible; everything else, no matter how improbable, is possible."

"You start with what's most probable and work backwards."

"Our engine instructor was this old sergeant, nasty and dirty but smart as a coyote. This guy drew a line on the blackboard when he taught diagnostics. On one side, he listed things that happen to engines from normal wear. On the other, everything else."

"Sarge whacked that side of the blackboard and shouted at us, 'What's on this side of the line? Goddamn stupid soldiers! Or your enemy!'"

Tacho slapped his thigh with his grimy hand for emphasis, "That old man whacked his blackboard every time he said 'your enemy.' It was his shorthand for everything in the world that ticked him off."

"His message stuck."

Tacho leaned gently against the doorframe and looked back toward the ranch house. "Sarge drummed one fact into us day after day. I can still hear him, 'When you find something on the far side of that line, and you've ruled out dumb ass soldiers, go after your enemy before you fix your engine, or it'll break the same way again and again and again.' He'd whack the board when he said 'again.'"

Tacho whacked his thigh again to convey the point.

"The day I left 'Nam, this old guy found me and shook my hand. He only had three fingers left. He told me, 'You're going back to the real war now, soldier; I won't be there to watch your ass so you gotta watch it yourself!'"

"That's the only time I saw him smile. I bet he's still at it, wherever the war is now."

Tacho finished his story, "That was what, twenty-five years ago? Damn good advice," he nodded thoughtfully.

Tacho seldom swore, I could see several reasons why this memory had stuck in his mind and I marveled at the Army's pedagogy.

The big man raised one eyebrow and folded his handkerchief carefully before slipping it back into his pocket. He picked up one of the ball bearings and rolled it between his thumb and forefinger, "This act was not dumb. Someone who knew what they were doing took the top off the carburetor and poured these fellas down the air intake."

He dropped the ball bearing onto my desk and it bounced back up and he caught it and slipped it back in his watch pocket. I winced at the sight of his bruised knuckles.

He waited for my reply. When I said nothing he raised his eyebrows and looked back at the kitchen.

"You're thinking Nora?" I queried him. "She's just a kid. What does she know about engines, and why on earth would she do something like that?"

“You tell me,” Tacho replied, his voice affable as if we’d been discussing melons in the garden. “Who else is there? She shows up, the truck dies. No one except you came up the driveway Saturday night and yesterday. With this smoke the whole range is closed. Rule out the impossible,” he reminded me. “Who’s left?”

“Let’s get to know her a bit,” he mused. “It’s lunchtime. I’d like to wash up and get some cream on these hands. How about we take back your kitchen while we still have the numbers on our side?”

Tacho smiled but he was dead serious. I concurred. We locked the office and strolled across the driveway, opened the screen door and stepped into the kitchen.

Nora was still seated at the table, leafing through a magazine. She looked up as we entered. “Rough morning?” she inquired, eyeing Tacho’s hands.

He smiled and took off his straw hat, hanging it carefully by the door before replying, “Yes, ma’am. Welcome to the Canciones.” He extended his hand despite the grime and after a second Nora got up and shook it. Then he continued to the sink and began to scrub, using a nail brush to carefully work all the dirt from his hands. Nora and I stood and watched.

After I moment, I broke the silence. “How about some lunch?” Hearing no reply from either Tacho or Nora, I stepped past her to the ice box and took out a chunk of pot roast wrapped in wax paper, a couple of withered tomatoes and a jar of mayonnaise. I drew a loaf of bread from the breadbox and detached the butcher’s knife and the bread knife from their magnetic strip on the wall above the drain board. I took the maple cutting board from its nail adjacent to the knife rack.

Tacho scrubbed and Nora stepped aside so I could set the beef on the board on the table. I sliced a few strips of beef and quartered the tomatoes. I put the beef back in the ice box and then sliced the bread, slathered on the mayo.

This completed the sandwiches. I cut each in two.

All the while, Tacho worked with his back to Nora and she watched the muscles in his shoulders coil and uncoil beneath his denim shirt. She hadn't spoken since her initial question.

I felt uncomfortable with the silence even though Tacho and I could work together all day and not talk much. I set the three sandwiches on plates on the table and poured water from a jar in the cooler into three tall glasses. I retrieved three blue bandana napkins from a high shelf.

Finally I broke the silence, "Luncheon is served, ladies and gentlemen; get it while it's hot. Or cold. As the case may be."

Tacho completed his task and dried his hands carefully. He smiled at us, took the knives from the cutting board and washed them with care, replaced them on their magnet.

We all sat down. Tacho took the head of the table and Nora and I sat across from one another.

Tacho sipped his water and bit into his sandwich. Although he had proposed the conversation, I realized I needed to start it. I smiled at Nora, "Andrea tells me you're ranch stock," I began.

She nodded and sucked her cheeks. "My father was a rancher up by the Grand Canyon. My mom left him and went back east when I was five. I stayed. I grew up on the ranch, so you could call me ranch stock."

"What's his name?" I stretched to be polite. "Maybe I know him. I get up there sometimes and we all hit the State Fair. You run cattle?

"Ran."

"He left the business?"

"Dead."

This stopped me. Tacho raised one eyebrow and continued to chew his beef. I picked up my sandwich and took a bite, but did not taste much.

Nora smiled a tight smile. She licked her lips and narrowed her eyes, glancing at Tacho, then fixing me. Smoke seeped in through the screen door and I cleared my throat. "I'm sorry for your loss," I managed.

"Me too." Her eyes were the color of mesquite ash; it was hard to tell where the whites ended and the pupils began.

She munched on her beef. "The summer I turned thirteen, my dad and I were riding up on Third Mesa when a storm came up. We got wet as eels and we set out to race back to the barn."

She took a drink from her glass and continued, "I had the faster horse and I was about fifty feet in front of him as we came into Headquarters. I heard this crash and the whole world turned to fire, and then I was sitting on the ground and my horse gone. My father had been struck square by lightning; it killed him and his horse instantly.

They were both lying there on the ground in the rain fifty feet back of me. It got me, too, but it just set my hair on fire; the downpour put it right out and my scalp wasn't even burned. It didn't affect my horse at all; except after that she was scared of her own shadow and everything in between."

"The ranch might have been mine but the bank took it and now it's condos. I went back East to live with my mom but that didn't work. I ran away. Then I spent some time in a special boarding school. I got my education but I never let them cut my hair. I checked out last year when I turned 22."

Now Tacho spoke. "I knew your parents," he began. "My father blacksmithed up north and I worked with him when I was in high school. We have family on the Rez."

Nora sucked her cheeks again and then smiled broadly at Tacho. "Yeah, I figured that out from what Andrea told me. Says you're a hunk!"

"How about you, old man?" she widened her eyes at me and I suddenly felt her bare foot slide up my calf.

I jerked back as if snakebit and her foot fell away. Her chair clattered and then she regained her balance. Her smile never wavered.

Tacho continued to munch calmly on his sandwich, his eyes on Nora.

"Nora, you're in the wrong place," I stammered. "I don't know what you came out here expecting, but we're busting our asses in this drought and Andrea led us to believe you'd lend us a hand!"

She continued to smile. "That's my specialty!"

Tacho sighed. He had finished half his sandwich. He stood up and laid his hand lightly on Nora's shoulder. "That rancher was Sam Hastings," he said softly. "I remember when the lightning got him. Everyone on the Rez knew him. We heard the story; it's actually woven its way into Our Story over the last ten years."

Tacho tightened his grip a bit on her shoulder and Nora's smiled faded a degree. "Actually, Sam's daughter was also killed by that lightning strike. They were riding side by side. A tragedy."

"So you're not quite what you claim to be."

"But you're in Our Story too, ma'am," Tacho continued, speaking softly but not moving his hand. I watched his finger tendons stand out a fraction as his grip tightened a little more.

"You were there that day, on a white Appaloosa mare, so the Story goes. So you're not Sam's daughter—you're his daughter's friend. You're the third person riding in that storm that day. No one, not even the elders, knew where you came from or where you went after the funeral."

"But you're part of the Story."

Nora's smile disappeared. Her eyes welled up. "I can't help it," she moaned.

Tacho nodded. He did not let go of her shoulder and I could see he was holding her in her seat. Her chair shook a bit as she strained to rise but she could not move an inch.

Tacho looked over to me. "Go get her backpack," he nodded in the direction of Andrea's room. "Don't look inside and don't touch the metal frame. Carry it by the strap and set it on the porch," he gestured toward the screen. "Miss Nora and I are going for a drive."

It took me less than a moment to retrieve the pack but when I returned Tacho and Nora were waiting in his pickup on the driveway. Nora opened her door and grabbed the pack with one hand and wrestled it onto the truck floor beneath her feet. Tacho had her other wrist pinned to the seat.

They drove off through the smoke, down the driveway, out of my sight. I remained on the porch.

I leaned on the post for a few minutes and then went back into the kitchen. I pitched the remains of the sandwiches into the garbage, washed all the plates and their glasses, and carried my glass back outside.

I drank the cold water. Sara and Andrea walked up the path from the barn, arm in arm, as they had when my daughter was small.

They greeted me in the shade of the porch. "Where's Nora? Andrea asked.

"She had to leave early," I replied. "One way ticket, nonrefundable."

Late that day Tacho returned. In the bed of his pickup he carried a Plymouth engine from a junkyard in town. That night, he pulled the ruined one from the truck and welded a new cross-member to the Dodge's frame. The new engine was a little shorter but he made it fit, and by the next afternoon the cowboys were hauling water again.

Eventually rain returned to the ranch, but Nora never did.

SOUND WATER

I angled the Jeep across the barrow ditch and parked by the gate to Pasture Four. I was early on purpose. This was one of my favorite spots, and whenever I had an excuse to come here I liked being alone for a few minutes.

Everything here seemed to fit: the mountain, the canyon, the way the wrinkled desert fanned out to the west like an old elephant's hide. It was always quiet right here, despite the wind up on the ridge. The fact that you could hear the wind in the distance made it even quieter.

Before long I heard her car, still a few miles below me. I could see the dust curl up off the road before I saw the car. I watched her come, curious where our meeting would lead.

Pasture Four was a dilemma. This close to the mountain, plenty of rain fell even in drought summers, so there was feed, but no water. We couldn't put cattle here unless we left the gates open, and still they overgrazed the other pastures rather than walk up here for good grass and then back to water. Bad for the cattle, bad for the land, and bad for my wallet. I was willing to give anything a try.

I don't know what I expected, but when her car got close enough to make out details I was surprised. An old Volvo, from the 1950's, before they got boxy; it was almost sleek. I couldn't remember having seen one out west, and I caught myself wondering if she'd driven it all the way from New York. I was a little reassured when I saw the Cattle Grower's Association logo in her front license plate slot. This might be an interesting conversation after all.

She stopped at the edge of the road and I walked across the barrow ditch and greeted her, "Right on time. Thanks for coming all this way. I'll pull through the gate and you can park where the Jeep is, and we can go in together, if that's okay with you."

She smiled and shook my hand through the window, and I could see that she fit this place just fine. I walked back, opened the gate and drove the Jeep through, then waited for her while she negotiated the barrow ditch. I could see why she liked the old Volvo. With high ground clearance with a short wheelbase, it managed the ditch as well as the Jeep; it could probably go anywhere it could get traction.

She thanked me and stepped over the bottom of the gate and walked around to the right side of the Jeep. She seemed about my daughter's age, clean faded Levi's and a tan chamois shirt tucked in under a beaded belt. She carried a black gym bag, which I supposed held her tools, whatever they might be.

She waited until I was back behind the wheel before she got in. She had been studying the mountain. As we started up the trail, I asked her what she saw.

"I can see why you called me," she said. "Water's going to be tough here. See those dikes?" She pointed up toward the ridge. "When these mountains were formed, the rocks that had been laid down over the ages got tilted on edge. Over the years, the rain in the lee of the ridge washed the loose dirt to form this fan. With the rain and the south face, all this soil is the main reason you get such good grass. But those dikes go all the way to the center of the earth, or they might as well, as far as ground water's concerned. We need to look for a crack."

I was impressed. "That makes sense," I said, "but what about the rain that falls here? Where does that water go?"

"Into the San Kino," she said. "Ground water flows just like runoff. Here and there, you'll find a lens, like a pothole under the soil, where it catches. There's always a few, even this close to the mountain. Some dowser'll get you to drill a well into one, and you'll get water for a couple of years, but then the well goes dry and your dowser's gone, too."

"Here's my deal." She turned toward me and her eyes were green as summer emeralds; they met mine as I glanced over at her in spite of the rough road. The Jeep hit a rock and I winced.

"I charge a hundred dollars to come and look. Another hundred if you decide to drill. If you hit water in less than fifty feet, we wait and see. Put a windmill on it. You'll need to go up higher than you usually do to catch the wind here."

"Two years from now, if it still flows at ten gallons a minute or better, you pay me five hundred dollars. If not, we're square: the stock that drank what water was in the lens will have paid for the windmill and trough."

"You can go deeper if you want; sometimes the lenses have a little crack that goes down to a stream and that's what I've picked up." She smiled again, straight white teeth in a tan face that fit as if she had been born right here.

I almost replied "You had me at hello," but she might have taken it the wrong way, so I just smiled back and said. "You know these mountains better than I do."

"I doubt that. I just know them different. You know where the cattle hide when the wind blows, like my dad. I could never find them, so he finally gave up on me as a rancher and sent me to college. I find water for him, too, but he won't admit it. He bought the ad for me in the Cattle Grower's program book at the Fair."

She turned her attention back to the mountain and we fell silent as we maneuvered the rocky trail toward the canyon that split the center of the pasture.

Then she said, "Hold it!" and I stopped the Jeep. "Look at that!"

She was already out of the Jeep and striding up the trail, then off to the right a bit to get a better view of whatever she'd seen. She was as excited as a hunter and if it had been November I'd have instinctively reached for my 30.30, convinced by her tone that she'd seen a big buck. Today, I had no idea what she was looking at, or even what she was looking for, but her excitement caught me and I followed her. The mountain looked just the same to me.

After about fifty feet she stopped and then trotted back to the Jeep, stepping around me like I was a tree in her path. She returned with her gym bag.

She kicked at the soil to smooth a place and then knelt down and unzipped the bag. I noticed her shoes. They were moccasins; not the cheap kind from the trading post but sturdy as boots, soft, laced up her leg past where I could see when she knelt down. She took several little wooden tubes out of the bag. At first, I thought it was some sort of fly rod that might collapse into a backpack, but it slid together to make a long fork.

"The elders still use a willow," she said, noticing my staring as she stood up. "But they dry out in a week or so. This is made from the heart of a cottonwood, and it's sealed with beeswax and fit so you can carry it without breaking and then put it together when you need it."

"It's three times longer than their willows, and three times stronger." She smiled again and her eyes lit up. "Or at least I believe it is, which is all that counts."

I still didn't know what she'd seen and apparently she wasn't going to tell me, so I settled back to watch, enjoying the quiet pasture. She walked a grid, watching of course for snakes, but concentrating on the tip of the fork, which balanced in the air about four feet in front of her. Her back was straight as an arrow and all kinds of feelings flowed across her face as if she were watching a movie, reacting to scene after scene. Sometimes, she frowned; and once she burst out laughing. I watched and was entertained, too, although I had no idea what she saw or sensed.

Her grid extended about a hundred feet in each direction. Time stood still: but thinking back, it might have been close to an hour. I felt happy. A flock of chickadees came and went from the mesquite tree whose shade I sought. I watched a lizard poke its striped head out of a split rock, test me, and, sensing no danger, go about its business.

No flies bothered me because no water could be found within five miles; but just as she came back down the trail a blue swallowtail butterfly fluttered into the shade and lit right on the toe of my boot. Motionless, we watched it together for a moment before it left us.

She packed her fork back into her bag and stood up. "If you drill where I stacked that quartz cairn, you'll hit twenty gallons a minute thirty feet down." She looked me right in the eye, not smiling at all. I knew she was certain, and that she was afraid I wouldn't believe her, or even just doubt a little and show this by my expression. That would be the end of our friendship.

But I did not doubt her at all, and, five years later, twenty gallons a minute flows as sure in drought years as in plenty. Calves from Pasture Four crowd sleek and fat across the scales each shipping day. Good for the land and for me, too.

She did smile when I wrote her the check for two hundred dollars before we got back into the Jeep. She folded it and slipped it into her hip pocket. We lingered, leaning on the fender a moment, soaking up the quiet. I was headed home to a noisy corral, and she, back over the horizon to wherever she and her Volvo spent the night.

We rattled back down the trail toward the gate. We were friends now, so I felt confident enough to ask the question that had been in the back of my mind since she first drove up and rolled down her window.

"How do you stay safe doing this kind of work way out in the middle of nowhere, a young woman alone meeting all kinds of men?"

"Well," she said, smiling a softer smile and letting her face show its memories, "my aunt taught me this work. She's a dowser, too, and her aunt before her, all the way back. Some call us water witches, but there's nothing magic about us. We're dowsers. We just know how to see. "

"When it comes to men, my aunt taught me how to see three things. I look for two of these before I even open the car window."

"First, are his pants tucked into his boots? If so, I drive right on by. He's from Texas and not worth the time to stop."

"If his pants are over his boots, I'll stop, but if he's wearing dark glasses, I'll talk through the window. I won't shake hands 'til I get out of the car and have a clear shot."

"Some younger men do wear shades, you know, it's a habit they pick up in school and they might still be okay."

"The third thing I check is his fingernails when we shake hands. I watch men's hands coming to mine and then meet their eyes when we shake. I won't shake hands with a man unless he takes off his glove; any decent man will, you know, even if it's December and the wind is howling."

"So I always see his nails. They've got to be clean or the business stops right there. I might make up an excuse, like 'I walked land like this a couple of years back and you're wasting your money, there's no water here.' I get back in my car and go draw a beer at the nearest crossroads gas station. I call my dad and tell him 'don't ever buy a horse from that fellow.' I drink my beer and send a prayer up to my aunt for these three things she taught me."

"She worked these ranches for fifty years and never had a problem. I've been at it five years now; I met my husband out on the Reservation a couple of years ago when his boss was looking for a well, just as you are."

"I've never taken a step away from my car in the desert with any man I didn't trust. Men are men, and most of them take a look, and I like that; but if I see any of those three signs, I look out for number one."

Now she smiled that full smile and touched my shoulder as I pulled up to the gate. "My husband was wearing dark glasses but his nails are gorgeous."

"I'll get the gate so you don't have to walk out and back twice."

I watched her Volvo until it was out of sight and the dust had settled. I went home and called my well man. Two years later to the day, I got a brief note from her, remembering the well, with a stamped return envelope for her five hundred dollars. I wrote the check and slipped it in the envelope before I left the post office. I drove up to Pasture Four and watched the high windmill turn, listening to the smooth soft murmur as water poured into the cement tank.

Everything fit, and I smiled.

BRANDING FIRE

Sara kindled the branding fire each day during spring roundup.

Tacho and I honed the roundup plan, and after thirty years of practice we needed only three cowboys to gather and brand more than 600 calves in less than a month.

We set out at dawn each morning with five fresh horses in the cattle truck. The cowboys followed in the Jeep, carrying several welded pipe fence sections for the branding lane in its bed. They towed a trailer that converted into the branding squeeze chute and table.

We didn't reconnect with Sara until mid-day. She spent the morning preparing for us. She and Tacho's wife Sofia cooked a big meal of stew, meat loaf or pot roast. They baked bread and stacks of cookies. They wrapped everything in newspaper or ice chests to keep it warm or cold and packed the meal in our battered old station wagon, along with plates, cups, the coffee pot and water cooler, a folding enamel table and camp stools.

Sara's goal was to arrive by midmorning in whatever pasture we were gathering and set her table near a windmill and corral.

There she built her fire.

March weather was generally dry and windy. Fires were easy to start but could get out of hand quickly. The mesquite brush and creosote were tinder-dry in the lowlands; in the foothills, the oak and pine forests were eager to burn.

We needed a big fire to make the heavy branding irons red hot, but we could never risk the fire's spread. Conscious of this danger, Sara's first task was to gather stones, make a big fire pit, and clear all the brush for twenty feet or so around it. She visited the corrals in January or February to gather wood and stones for her fire pits, but wind or flash floods destroyed her handiwork more often than not. Other years, campers or smugglers took all her wood, so when March arrived she had to start from scratch.

Tending the branding fire was not an easy job, but she performed it to perfection day after day, year after year.

While Sara built her fire, we moved cattle from the four corners of the pasture toward the corrals. It took three of us to assemble a herd and get it headed toward water; from that point one cowboy could follow the cows and calves alone.

Most pastures contained or shared a set of three linked corrals with a slanted chute at one end for the cattle truck. The outermost corral was a big holding trap of two or three acres fenced with barbed wire. This trap generally had a water trough at one corner where it joined the two smaller corrals, which were built with rough timbers nailed to railroad ties set in the ground, or, on the older part of the ranch, mesquite logs.

We left the gate from the trap to the pasture open year 'round so the cattle got used to going in for water. By the time Spring arrived, the cows had forgotten the trap had a gate and streamed in with their calves; the cowboy who followed them was able to dismount and close the gate.

Meanwhile, Sara opened the gate by the trough, which led into the next corral. The herd's inclination to spook away from her and escape back into the pasture was thwarted by the cowboy on his horse at the closed gate.

If all went according to plan, the cows and calves turned back by the trough and crowded into the middle corral. Sara learned to climb fences fast to get away from the cows; they viewed people on foot as a threat to their calves. She wore leather gloves and heavy boots and paid particular attention in the old mesquite corrals: good habitat for snakes, pack rats, black widow spiders and other desert creatures she'd rather not encounter.

After the cowboy enclosed the cattle in the middle corral, he reopened the main gate to the trap in time for the next herd. Then he slipped into the middle corral and pushed the cattle forward again as Sara opened the gate to the innermost corral. This strategy emptied the middle one by the time the next herd, followed by the next cowboy, arrived by the trough in the trap.

All morning this process continued. On a good day no one got trampled, and by noon most of the pasture's cows and calves were settled in the innermost corral, near the windmill, with plenty of water for all in the tank at its base.

The fire was hot, dinner was ready, and the branding irons were starting to glow.

Some days only the cowboys and Tacho and I gathered around the branding fire. However, it was not unusual for visitors to come to spend the afternoon by the corrals and watch us work.

Branding defined ranch life. One year a newspaper in the state capital ran a Sunday supplement feature entitled "Experience Real Working Ranches!" with a map and guide, advertising ranches as though we some sort of exotic theme park.

The article irritated me, as it did most ranchers, but at the same time we were heartened that the editor recognized that ranches were still a cornerstone of the state's economy, that ranchers worked hard. We knew our product fed people in eastern cities where the only cowboys were on cigarette billboards, and hoped the editor recognized that our reality was different from that of his readers in those cities.

Visitors to our branding fires generally fell into one of three groups: horse traders came to watch the cowboys work the herd with their cutting horses; artists came with their cameras and palettes and notebooks; animal rights activists came to harass us.

Sara welcomed all guests to her fire, but she made it clear that the hearth was hers.

One Friday that March the planets aligned, and Tacho and I discovered lots of all three categories of visitors waiting when we rode in behind the last few cows and calves from the far corner of the pasture. Six unfamiliar cars were parked in the shade cast by several big palo verde trees past the corrals. A gaggle of new white cowboy hats bobbed around the fire pit. Cameras bristled on the cattle truck running board and a couple of easels sprouted by the chute.

Our three cowboys were leaning against the truck fender, talking to a couple of leggy young women dressed in T-shirts and shorts and Keds. A third woman with a blond braid that reached her belt paced between the girls and the fire pit. She wore jeans and boots and a denim shirt, and her weathered straw hat looked more at home than the new Stetsons.

A horse trader had his thumb in the mouth of the horse we called Blockhead, checking his teeth. The horse was tied to the corral, his ears laid back; his cowboy, who should have been keeping an eye on him, jawed with the girls in the Keds. Blockhead was known to take a chunk out of people who fiddled with him; watching the horse trader I was conflicted what to hope for.

Tacho and I pushed the cows and calves past the first trough and then into the corral. No one bothered to open the gates for us; we did so from horseback. We closed the gate behind the cattle, dismounted and tied our horses to the corral next to Blockhead.

"Here we go." I said to Tacho. He raised his eyebrows and took a long drink from his canteen.

I searched the crowd for Sara. I saw her by the fire.

"Get your hand out of my horse's mouth," I growled to the horse trader. "He doesn't know where that hand has been." I glared at the cowboys by the truck and stalked across the bare ground toward the fire pit.

Sara stood up and turned to greet me. "I've got it," she said quietly.

I raised my voice, "Who are all these people?" I swung my arm in a wide arc to take in the girls, the fence hangers, the spotless Stetsons around the fire. "Where did they all come from? What are they doing here?"

"I've got it!" she hissed. "You get yourself some dinner from that pot on the table and go protect your poor cowboys from those sweeties in the shorts."

"When I need you I'll find you! Your irons are hot—you keep cool—get something to eat and get on with your branding."

Sara glared at me and I got the message.

I ladled a helping of beef stew onto a big enamel plate and drew a cup of coffee from the crock. I heaped a couple of pieces of bread on top and balanced it across to the cattle truck. I set it on the running board on the shady side.

"Fellas!" I shouted to the cowboys. They jumped back from the fender and sidled over, followed by the Keds and the blonde in the boots.

I tipped my hat to the ladies as if I'd learned it just so in rancher charm school. The T-shirt clad Keds smiled but the third looked at me hard, her arms folded across her denim shirt. "Gentlemen," I said to the cowboys, "would you care to introduce your friends to your boss?"

"Um, sure," the cowboy we called Teeth responded. His face turned red as the stew on my dinner plate. "This here is Judi, with an 'i.' And Hillary." He looked unsure of the blonde.

I took pity on him and extended my hand to her. "And you would be?" I smiled my sweet charm school smile.

Several seconds passed. I continued to meet her eyes. She uncrossed her arms and extended her hand. Her nails were chewed to the quick so I was careful not to squeeze too hard.

"My name is Morgan Quicksilver," she replied evenly. "Reporter for the *Daily Sentinel*. We're doing a series of articles on the 'Farm Broccoli, Not Babies' movement."

"You've heard of them?" She raised one eyebrow.

"Yes, ma'am." I replied. It was hard to miss the cute calf surrounded by the words *Babies Need Love* on the Keds girls' t-shirts.

It was a familiar logo I'd seen at booths at the County Fair and in the halls of the statehouse.

I continued to smile but I held onto Morgan's hand a moment longer than was really necessary. I reflected to myself that she could be pretty if she would stop frowning. I could see why Teeth and his buddies were distracted.

"Your wife is so sweet!" The Ked named Judi gushed, breaking the tension. "She offered us lunch as soon as we got here, and I would have taken some, it smells so good, but, we don't eat babies, so I just took some bread and some Jello."

"And about a dozen cookies!" Hillary smiled at me too. Even Morgan relaxed a little at this and I could see some potential.

I let go of her hand. She extracted a note pad from her hip pocket and from her braid a gnawed yellow pencil that appeared to have been sharpened with a pocketknife.

Her nails were evidently not the only thing Morgan chewed.

"Well, that's nice." I replied to the Keds. "I wouldn't worry about the beef in the stew," I went on. "That old girl wasn't one of our babies; she was a milk cow that had a good life in a nice pasture. She went dry, hurt her hip so it locked up. She would have gone to the slaughterhouse or died in her tracks before long if we didn't take her from her pain."

I looked at Morgan. "We know how slaughter houses are and I can assure you, that old cow died with dignity, and I'm sure she'd be okay with us eating her today. We liked her and we like all our babies, too. We don't eat them either."

Thirty years ago I would have added "except for their balls" but Sara had taught me a bit of tact in that time, so I kept the thought to myself. "We do have to brand them today, though, and..." I began.

"Oh, yes!" Judi jumped in before I could finish. "Your wife sat us all down and told us all about branding. She told us about your MW brand and what it stood for."

"My Way," I thought dourly to myself, but I kept my peace.

"That's right," Hillary chimed in. "Your wife said it doesn't really stand for anything special but it means in a pinch you can use the same iron for the top and the bottom of the brand."

Teeth had found his voice again. "Miss Sara called us over as soon as we got the cows in and introduced us to these ladies," he prattled.

"She said to show them around the corrals, so we did". Teeth's face had faded back to pink under his straw hat. "She's talkin' to that other group there now. They did eat well," he added. "And we're done eatin', too."

"Well, hospitality is Miss Sara's gift." I nodded to Teeth and the other cowboys. "You fellas get on with your work. You know what needs doing. I'll be along as soon as I finish my dinner."

I looked pointedly at the three men. "Whoever is riding Blockhead, go have a word with Tacho before you get back into the corral." I met each of their eyes and one of them turned as pale as Teeth had been red. They sauntered off in the direction of their horses, tied to the corral fence back of the truck.

Now it was Morgan's turn, "What do you think of 'Farm Broccoli, Not Babies,' sir?" she began. "Will they put people like you out of business? How will you prevent them from dousing your branding fires?"

Her pencil was poised.

I held up my hand to stop her, but in a gentle way. "Branding is painful," I acknowledged. "If you or I were getting branded, maybe because of our religion or our politics, or because we were a man or a woman, it would be torture--an evil act."

"That does happen in parts of our world, you know," I looked Morgan in the eye. "Miss Quicksilver, I've read the series you wrote about trafficking in women, sex slavery and so on; bad men branding women as if they were their property."

Morgan bit her pencil tip and fiddled with her notebook. The Keds stared.

"You write well," I went on. "I believe your series won an award for your paper?"

Morgan's eyes darted from the Keds to the cowboys and back to me. She hadn't written anything on the pad.

She nodded.

"What are you men waiting for?" I snapped at the cowboys, who were drifting close again.

They scrambled away toward the corral and I turned my attention back to Morgan. "People can be animals, but the opposite isn't necessarily true," I continued. I pointed to the herd milling behind the fence, "Beef cattle like these are the product of a thousand years of selective breeding. We made them what they are; now we're obliged to protect them from predators."

"From reading your series, I know I don't need to tell you that wolves and lions aren't the big predators: it's people. Rustlers, for one. Dumb hunters who don't know a buck from a bull, for another."

"Then, there's your readers, who I'd wager are generally pretty ignorant about ranch life." I pointed at Morgan's pad, "If you're going to write something, make damn sure it's true. The fact is, with the calves, if it's done right, branding takes about three seconds and a minute later their mothers are licking them and loving them and giving them their supper."

"Did my wife tell you what a ''maverick' calf is?" I asked pointedly, "One that we fail to brand?"

"Oh, yes!" Judi jumped in before Morgan could reply. "And she told us rustlers prowl around looking for mavericks, for their skin to make perfect soft leather coats."

"If they find one they shoot its mommy right in front of it and then they skin the baby alive," she finished her story, widening her eyes so I'd know she'd learned well. She had put on plenty of eyeliner that morning and her brows looked to be painted on as well.

"That does happen," I nodded, my eyes following Morgan's expression. In contrast to the Keds, she wore no makeup at all. Had my tide turned with her? I said a silent prayer of thanksgiving for Sara and her branding fire.

Remembering Sara's advice, I decided I'd better let the conversation go for now. "If you'll excuse me?" I said to the Keds and the reporter, who had yet to scribble a word.

"My dinner is getting cold and I've got a full afternoon ahead of me. You're welcome to stay and watch but I would take it quite seriously if you were to say anything critical to my men about their work. They depend on their paychecks and this is the only work they know."

"They're professionals. It would be a shame if they were to lose their jobs over something that doesn't really concern them."

I smiled and looked pointedly at Morgan. She knit her brow again but it wasn't quite a frown.

"My wife can fill in the details," I finished. "I'll be right here if you need me." I touched the tip of my hat brim and sat down on the running board. I balanced my plate on my lap and unwrapped my fork and knife from the heavy blue bandana Sara provided for napkins. I sipped my coffee. It was still nice and hot.

The three women understood the conversation was over. Judi and Hillary nodded eagerly and the corners of Morgan's mouth turned up ever so slightly. A hint of straight white teeth touched her lower lip. She nodded, too, and slipped her pad in her pocket and her pencil in her braid.

The three stepped gingerly back toward the fire pit, avoiding a sizable pile of manure Blockhead had dropped as his cowboy led him by, headed for the gate to the corral. The cowboy came back and took the short-handled shovel from its slat on the rack of the cattle truck. He cleared the manure and put the shovel back. He did not look at me.

Tacho brought his dinner over and squatted in the shade of the truck. "Blockhead's still all ours," he reported. "And one cowboy's a little smarter than he was."

"Still two to go," he laughed. "Next lesson will be on picking girlfriends!" I joined his laughter, wiping my mouth with the bandana. We heard snippets of conversation from the fire pit. The mesquite smoke smelled sweet; the irons were hot.

It was time to brand.

Success depended on our horses. Several years earlier the horse we called Blockhead arrived unexpectedly at the ranch, thrown in for free with two horses we bought through a broker in Texas. At first we just called him Tex, but soon his many bad behaviors earned him his new moniker.

He was hard to load in a truck or trailer, laying back his ears and shying away from the gate. Once loaded he didn't want to get out. He kicked anyone who walked behind him; bit other horses and the occasional careless cowboy. He would walk straight into a mesquite thicket rather than follow the trail around it.

All in all, Blockhead had a bad attitude and seemed to enjoy it.

Blockhead's skill as a cutting horse more than made up for his shortcomings. He was the best cutting horse I had ever seen. Day after day during Spring roundup, Blockhead's unique gift was the key to a successful afternoon; a joy to watch for cattlemen and dudes alike.

Forty-two cows and thirty-seven calves milled in the corral. The cowboys on their horses began to separate them. Blockhead darted quickly between a cow and her calf, startling them in opposite directions; the two other cowboys kept them moving, widening the gap.

The calves were easy enough to control, but the cows resisted. The cowboys' job was to push the separated cows out of the corral as quickly as possible. Often a cow broke back toward the calves, but Blockhead had an instinctive ability to anticipate her every move, and positioned himself in her path whichever way the increasingly angry and frustrated cow turned.

The horse was fearless.

His rider didn't have to touch the reins; in fact, it was all his cowboy could do to stay in the saddle as Blockhead wheeled to and fro, pushing the cow back toward the gate. The second cowboy kept the growing herd of calves together at the branding end of the corral, while the third worked the gates as cows straggled reluctantly back into the middle corral and then through to the trap.

From that vantage point they jostled one another to get as close as they could to the fence and angle for a view, bawling to their calves.

Once about half the calves were separated from their mothers Tacho and I began to brand. Tacho waded into the calves and muscled a few at a time into a narrow lane made with the portable fence sections the cowboys had brought in the Jeep.

This lane led to the branding chute, which could be tipped on its side to become a table. Its wheels folded up so that it rested flat on the ground. When the lane was filled with calves, Tacho opened the back of the chute and the first calf rushed in, glimpsing an escape route.

At this point, timing was everything. Tacho dropped the gate behind the calf and I closed the gate at the front of the chute. The calf's momentum carried its head through a big collapsing triangle in the gate and I swung a lever down to hold it firmly without injuring it. Another lever allowed me to gently secure the calf between the chute's metal sides.

Tacho reached over the top and vaccinated the calf for blackleg while I dehorned it and cauterized the bleeding with a red-hot flat iron from the branding fire.

Then I pulled a third bar to swivel the whole chute into a horizontal position with the calf safely cradled. Tacho tethered the calf's front and back hooves and pulled his lariats tight to spread the calf out flat on its right side. The top side of the chute swung away so the calf lay before me on a table.

In this position I branded every calf.

Tacho castrated the bull calves. He made a tiny slit with his razor-sharp pocket knife, pulled their testes from their scrotums with a stainless steel hook, clipped them off and dropped them into a stainless steel bowl to save and cook as "mountain oysters."

Our visitors followed each step of this process, occasionally snapping pictures. For the most part Tacho and I ignored them and focused on our work.

When we had visitors, Sara made a point to engage them in conversation during lunch before the branding started. Although she appeared to keep the topics light, she used this time to judge who might be responsible enough to be an iron runner.

When there were no visitors Sara performed this job herself, but she was always grateful to find help. The branding irons were heavy, and it was tiring work that continued without a break until all the calves were branded.

In the rare instance when no wind blew, we could set the chute close enough that I could grab irons right from the fire; but most days, the risks fire and wind posed to the calves and the branders required that Sara kindle it at least twenty or thirty feet from the chute.

The iron runner's job was to take a red-hot branding iron from the fire pit and carry it quickly to me before it cooled, stand aside as I branded the calf, and then run it back to the fire without branding anyone or anything else along the way.

The whole branding process required three irons in proper sequence. First, I used the flat iron to cauterize the horn bud wounds, followed by the M and then the W for the brand on the calf's left hip,

M
W

If we had capable visitors at the branding fire, Sara would recruit three strong agile people who took the job of iron runner as seriously as surgical nurses in an operating room. As I had told the young women, it took about three seconds to brand each calf, but those seconds were exacting lest the iron slip and the brand smear.

Each brand seemed to take an eternity.

I understood why branding captivated people from the city. I grew up on the ranch and had seen it hundreds of times, but it still stirred my soul each time I held the hot iron against the calf's bare flank, squinting as the smoke curled up into my eyes, smelling the unexpectedly sweet aroma of burning hair and flesh.

Over the years I came to believe that the smell of the branding evoked ancient memories, hard-wired into our cells, like the rattle of a rattlesnake or the sight of a forest ablaze.

I couldn't imagine trusting a person who liked the smell of branding, but nevertheless the ritual drew visitors to the fire pit year after year. Some urbanites hung on the fences and watched the cutting horses do their job; co-eds from the University came to flirt with the cowboys; a few serious students of ranch life stayed close to the fire and chute to watch our art with the iron and the blade.

The smell was part of the work and the work was real. The calves moaned and Tacho smeared their wounds with bright purple iodine; we tipped them back up to the vertical position, and with three quick levers released them.

They ran bawling past the corral to find their mothers, who called to them from the water trough in the big trap. A cowboy stood by a small gate in the lower half of the fence near where the trap met the first corral, parting it just enough to let each calf squeeze through and race to its mother.

By this time Tacho had another calf in the branding chute.

Even though it had been years since I took over the branding from my father (and thereby lost my opportunity to watch), I knew the scene by the outer trough well; the relieved cow licking her baby from head to tail, cleaning the wounds, and then turning sideways to present her udder to her calf; the mother and child rejoined by the ancient ritual of love, the warm milk flowing.

All afternoon the herd of cows nursing calves grew, the mothers curling their heads back to lick the fresh brands while the nursing calves' tails swirled as if on swivels.

Meanwhile, the herd of anxious waiting cows grew ever smaller. It became easy to identify six cows who did not have calves. They stood aside from both herds, wandering up and down the trap, hoping to get back into the pasture.

Teeth came by the fire to report to Sara that five of these cows were dry, but that one had a full bag. Sara agreed with his suggestion to let the lactating cow back into the pasture and to follow her; she could be expected to go to her calf. Perhaps it was hidden somewhere as a doe will hide her fawn, and Teeth could rope the calf and bring it in across his pommel to get it branded.

If it had been stillborn, he could at least find its body before the buzzards did and bury it before dark.

We would bring the five dry cows home with us in the cattle truck for some hormone tests at Headquarters. They might get another chance to breed and calve next year, but if the test results showed them sterile, they'd be sold at auction next week.

The afternoon waned and the sun sank toward the western mountains. We were down to one heifer calf on the branding table and two bull calves in the lane.

Tacho had a break from his castrating duties for a few moments while I branded the heifer. He stood between the two calves in the lane. He and the little bulls were exhausted and all leaned against the fence, resting while I took care of the heifer. I was bone tired too.

Tacho took off his gloves and scratched one calf's back until it shivered with pleasure; he let the other suck on his finger: no milk, but still good for the calf. It reduced its anxiety at being separated from its mother for so long.

They were just babies and it was clear that Tacho loved them. So did I. I finished the dehorning, cauterized the bleeding corners of the heifer's white face and gave the flat iron back to the runner, then smeared the smoking wounds with iodine. I tipped the calf up on her side and with a wave to Tacho to stay put, tethered her front and back hooves myself and pulled her little body tight, still on the table. I vaccinated her.

I turned to take the "M" from the iron runner.

It was Morgan. She held the iron in gloved hands; for half a second I thought she had stolen an iron and aimed to brand me, but then I saw the big red "S" stitched on the backs of her gloves and realized they were Sara's, loaned to Morgan for this job. She held out the cool curled end of the red-hot iron to me and met my eyes straight on. "Take it!" she shouted. "It gets cold fast and it takes longer if it starts to cool!"

She was right. I took the iron and held it steady against the calf's hip for a second. The brand took so fast I was able to flip the iron over and make the "W" before it cooled at all. In two seconds we were done. I returned the iron to Morgan and waved off the other runner waiting with the hot "W". He saw what I had done and trotted back to the fire to return his iron to the coals.

Morgan and I stood alone by the tethered calf.

His back to us, Tacho stared off to the west as though he had never seen a sunset before, his finger in the next calf's mouth.

I gave Morgan a quizzical look. I started to stay something but she held one gloved forefinger up to her mouth, keeping the still-hot iron safe aside in her other hand. "When you're done," she said. She turned and trotted back to the fire. I watched Sara greet her, take the iron from her hand and the gloves, one by one. She squeezed the younger woman's shoulder once and set the gloves on a rock by the pit.

"Hey, Boss," I heard Tacho as if from a vast distance. "You gonna let that heifer go so we can get these two boys back to their mama? They're twins. Old 750 gave us twins again!"

I snapped out of my trance and smeared iodine on the brand. I loosened the heifer's hooves, lowered her to the ground, relaxed the squeeze, released her head and opened the front of the chute. I watched her run back toward the trough. Two cows waited by the gate. One was a horned cow that I recognized in an instant. She was eleven years old, older than we usually kept cows.

We kept 750 an extra year because she had calved every year and given us a set of twins when she was six. I smiled, seeing the one old cow still waiting for her twins as the heifer started to nurse on the other cow by the fence.

I felt a sting of tears in my eyes; they were not from the branding fire smoke. I didn't hide them from Tacho.

Tacho pulled the rope to open the chute and pushed in the first of the two twin calves. He leaned over and called to me above the clatter as I caught the calf's head in the gate, "What do you think we don't cut these two? Maybe they've got a gene for twins they could throw to heifer calves? We could use a couple of new bulls either way, and if it's true, when we're old we'll have a ranch full of twins.

I nodded. "Works for me," I responded. "We've got plenty of oysters for the crowd by the fire."

I decided not to de-horn these two little bulls. Old 750 was a Registered Hereford; her sons would keep their horns and stay on the ranch this fall. We would register them and braise their numbers onto their horns when they were two years old. Maybe we would take them to the State Fair and win a pair of blue ribbons. I could see the future unfold.

I shouted to Sara, "Keep the flatiron; these guys are staying. Send me the six."

She rolled her eyes as if she hadn't been doing this for thirty springs. "You sure what year this is? Make sure you keep it right side up, cowboy!" She grinned and turned back to the fire, shaking the coals to make sure the iron wrought into a six (or a nine) got hot.

We vaccinated and branded the two bulls. I added a six brand on their left shoulders so we could identify their age from afar all their lives. One after another they raced back to their mother, the only cow waiting, silhouetted against the fading light.

Teeth had followed the lonely wet cow, found her stillborn calf and buried it, using the shovel from the truck. All the other wet cows were back in the pasture with their calves. The dry cows were loaded in the cattle truck, the branding irons cooling in the water trough by the windmill.

Most of our visitors departed, including the horse trader. Morgan, the girls in the Keds and a couple of the runners lingered by the fire.

The old cattle truck wheezed to life and rattled off toward Headquarters, followed by the Jeep pulling the chute. Whichever cowboy's day it was would come back in the truck in an hour or so for Tacho and me and the horses.

Tacho I rested on folding camp chairs by the fire. Sara invited her remaining guests to take a seat. She passed around a jug of cold cider and tin cups.

We sipped our cider in silence as daylight wrinkled its way up the eastern mountains. Way off in the valley, the first lights twinkled in town.

Morgan sat next to me. The two Keds had donned hooded sweatshirts over their logo'ed t-shirts. Their sweats were inside out and I suspected they too bore logos.

I started the conversation. "Thank you all for your help today. We got the whole pasture gathered and branded and twin bull calves to boot. No one got hurt. No one got into a cactus and my cowboys are still single and sober."

"We're grateful to all of you."

I smiled at the two girls huddled in their shorts and sweatshirts. Away from the fire it was growing cold fast.

I addressed them, "It's Friday night. Two of those gents you were chatting with will be heading to town with their pay in their pockets as soon as they can get to the bunkhouse and shower and change. Their buddy will be back here to take care of the horses and bring us home, so he won't get going 'til ten or so."

"But that's early for you youngsters."

I grew serious. "Take a piece of advice from an old man. Put those sweatshirts on right side out. They've got your brand on them. It's not our brand, but if you're going to spend time on a ranch there's something you need to know: people worth a damn ride for their brand."

The Keds looked at me and then at Morgan. She had a mesquite twig in her hand and was fiddling with a fading ember in the fire pit. She hooked it and drew it out.

The two girls looked back at me, waiting to hear what came next.

I continued, "I'm familiar with your organization and I don't disagree with you about pigs and vealers. It's wrong for a calf not to run with its mother. It hurts the calf and it hurts the cow, too."

"Did you see that one mournful wet cow left alone at the end of the day? Her grief affects the whole herd."

The girls nodded tentatively and I warmed to my topic. "We keep pigs at the ranch, but not the way those confinement farms do. A pig is a clean animal if it has the chance. So as far as the vealers and pigs go, I'm with you."

"In any case, what I think shouldn't be your concern. You need to be proud of your brand and ride for it whether folks around you agree or not. That's part of this life. Good ranchers will respect you even where we disagree. The others don't matter: they're just politicians."

"In our culture people eat meat. We provide it for them, just as women and children in some sweatshop in Asia provided with you those sweatshirts. It's our living."

"We're all bound together in this crazy world and there's lots I don't know. My wife here taught me most of what I do know and Tacho taught me the rest."

"This I know: if you plan to hang around ranches, ride for your brand."

Hillary and Judi looked relieved. They stood up and stepped away from the fire, peeled off their sweatshirts, reversed them, and returned. As I suspected, they bore the logo.

Tacho braided his ever-present lariat. The two iron runners—artists from up north, Sara had told me—poked at the fire and sipped their cider.

I turned my attention to Morgan.

"Now, tell me," I smiled at her. "What's your brand? You said 'when you're done' to me an hour or so ago. Now I'm done."

"Well," she started, "I write for the *Sentinel* so I guess you could say that paper's my brand."

"But you were right about our readers. They don't really give a damn about ranch life, or anything else that doesn't fit their frame. That paper exists to sell ads and those ads sell cars and lingerie. They don't inform anyone about anything I really care for."

"We journalists are like the tail on a lizard! The cat whacks it, and off it comes."

"Advertisers are the cats in my business."

She looked around the circle to gauge our response, checking if she should trust us if she went on. Judi and Hillary perched on their stools, eyes eager. The rest of us nodded to Morgan.

Morgan bit at a raw finger and then continued, "You mentioned my story about Nigeria and Italy. It won us a plaque on the wall but it cost us $5,000 per day in advertising. The travel agents squawked, and then the editor of the travel section had a little talk with the publisher."

"Next morning, my editor is cleaning out her desk and I'm on fluff for the rest of my life."

“Not that you’re fluff, girls,” she said quickly to the Keds. “But your story’s going to run in the ‘color’ section on a Saturday, if you get my drift. If they find someone to write it. I couldn’t get my first sentence down after I held that iron.”

Morgan looked ruefully at her fingertips and then fiddled with the pencil in her braid. “Anyway, after my editor carried her box out, she came back and hung a black velvet ribbon on that award plaque over my desk. She gave me a hug and that’s the last I saw her. She’s gone back east; I’m the only desert rat left in the newsroom. That’s why they gave me this story.”

Morgan sighed. “I want to write the truth, so what do I write about today? And who will read it? My assignment was to write something light for the big company back east that owns the paper; make this broccoli bit look foolish or noble, or whatever it is.”

“But what is it?” Morgan looked at the Keds. They smiled uncertainly at her. She had left them in her tracks.

“I don’t know,” Morgan answered her own question. “I don’t eat veal, either, but this isn’t about veal. Or it’s about more than veal. Like I say, I’m looking for truth. It seems simple enough, but then when you try to write it down, it gets more complicated.

Morgan chewed the end of her mesquite twig for a moment and fiddled with her ember, now black. She pushed it back into the fire.

Her eyes met mine in the fading glow, “This fire is true. Your wife is true. Even those cowboys, chewing tobacco, tugging at their crotches when they think we aren't looking; and that loony horse that tried to bite me: they're all truer than what I do for a living right now."

Her ember caught again and flared. "I grew up in this state, for Christ sake. I remember when the *Sentinel* was a NEWSpaper."

"I'm going crazy at that friggin' rag but I have to pay my bills and this is the only work I know."

Morgan fumed. Sara suddenly tossed a donut hole across the fire pit, and despite the gathering darkness, Morgan caught it. Her ragged hands were that quick. She smiled ruefully at Sara.

"A girl can change her brand, you know." Sara reminded her. "You ran that iron pretty well today. Maybe you should get to know some of those cowboys a little better."

The rest of us listened as Sara continued, "Morgan, I came out here thirty years ago to marry that character sitting next to you. I didn't know a fencepost from a yucca tree then, but I've managed."

"It's not the work you know that matters. It's the work that knows you. Your work is looking for you. My work found me when I came up that dirt road out there one day with some guy I sat next to in Econ 101 Class at Cornell." Sara pointed toward Headquarters, far upslope from our fire, where a tiny light flickered in a canyon cleft against the fading foothills.

Home.

Sara lowered her voice, speaking directly to Morgan, "I'd never been west of Lake Erie. I was going to be an I-banker in New York like the rest of my family."

"Then this fire found me. Your fire will find you. You write beautifully, Morgan."

"Even more importantly, as you yourself said, what you write rings true."

"Maybe that's your brand. Somewhere, someone knows that and they're waiting for you to claim it."

"Look at it this way," Sara continued. She picked up her leather gloves from the flat rock at the lip of the fire pit and pulled them on against the gathering chill. "Part of this country is still open range. Once we're all done branding, all of us ranchers will run some of our cattle out there; come shipping day, we each claim our own."

"There are plenty of folks left in this world who will claim your brand of writing. Don't spend too much time defining exactly what your brand means. Those who see it will know what it means if they take the time to know you. Stick to your own brand, even if you're on the open range and no other brands match it. That's the whole point of 'branding'."

"And stop chewing pencils. They have lead in them, you know!"

Sara laughed in the firelight and after a few seconds, Morgan laughed too. She was indeed beautiful. She tossed the donut hole back across the fire pit at Sara. Sara caught it in one gloved hand. She was quick, too.

Morgan sends us a post card from time to time. Her books are published in Europe and she lives there now.

Once she sent us a picture clipped from an Oslo newspaper. Despite her short hair and long nails, we recognized her smile. She was accepting an award from a man dressed formally in tails. A large crowd beyond them stood and clapped.

Truth.

Acknowledgements

I owe a debt of gratitude to many people, without whom I could not have written these stories.

I thank my brother and sisters who protected me throughout my childhood. My first grade teacher, Mrs. Hughes, taught me to read; and my third grade teacher, Mrs. Hadley, encouraged me to channel my fierce chaotic energy into story-telling. I am grateful to them. I had wonderful role models as a child: Gilbert Garcia, Pat Stevenson, Keith and Bobbie Walden, Leota Moore; others too numerous to name. They noticed and cared about the strange but lovable child who hid behind many masks.

I left the desert in 1963, but the desert never left me. Mentors guided me with patience and love. Red Hinkley, Jane Smith and Mary Jo Adams set an example for integrity at work; at home my wife Alice, my daughters Amelia and Lisa, and their husbands, Graham and Matt, sustain me.

I read lots, and I am indebted to many authors who took the risk of putting their hearts on the page for me to treasure. Four have been as prophets: Edward Abbey, Wendell Berry, Cormac McCarthy, and Meg Wheatley.

I'm grateful to the citizens of Patagonia, Arizona, especially George R. Proctor, for their hospitality.

Finally, I'm eternally thankful for the skill of Valori Treloar, M.D. and Karen Dudich, M.D. who kept me alive long enough for a few stories to tumble out of my head. Plenty more stories rattle around up there, like a long freight train laden with spools of rusted barbed wire, the engineer squinting through fog and drifting sand to seek the switch to the westbound spur, praying it is still open.

-Craigville, MA, 2008-